THE CALLING CARD IS DEATH...

He walked forward and after a few steps could see a bundled figure backed up to the fence. Big enough to be Ernst Rutzmann, its posture was one of casual slumping against the fence. Two more steps and the man approaching the gate knew something was wrong. Now he ran forward. It was Rutzmann. Eyes wide open and staring. A frightful grimace covered his face. His top coat was damp with moisture, soaked with fresh blood. The crimson stain came from three ghastly wounds. A trio of spiked stakes had pierced his chest from behind when he was lifted and impaled on the fence.

NICK CARTER IS IT!

"Nick Carter out-Bonds James Bond."
—*Buffalo Evening News*

"Nick Carter is America's #1 espionage agent."
—*Variety*

"Nick Carter is razor-sharp suspense."
—*King Features*

"Nick Carter is extraordinarily big."
—*Bestsellers*

"Nick Carter has attracted an army of addicted readers . . . the books are fast, have plenty of action and just the right degree of sex . . . Nick Carter is the American James Bond, suave, sophisticated, a killer with both the ladies and the enemy."
—*The New York Times*

From The Nick Carter Killmaster Series

Revenge of the Generals
The Man Who Sold Death
Temple of Fear
The Liquidator
The Nichovev Plot
The Judas Spy
Time Clock of Death
Under the Wall
The Jerusalem File
The Filthy Five
The Sign of the Cobra
Six Bloody Summer Days
The Z Document
The Ultimate Code
The Green Wolf Connection
The Katmandu Contract
The Night of the Avenger
Beirut Incident

Dedicated to The Men of the
Secret Services of the
United States of America

A Killmaster Spy Chiller

THE NOWHERE WEAPON

CHARTER
NEW YORK

A DIVISION OF CHARTER COMMUNICATIONS INC.
A GROSSET & DUNLAP COMPANY

THE NOWHERE WEAPON
Copyright © 1979 by The Condé Nast Publications, Inc.

All rights reserved, including the right to reproduce this book or portions thereof in any form.

"Nick Carter" is a registered trademark of The Condé Nast Publications, Inc., registered in the United States Patent Office.

Charter Books
A Division of Charter Communications, Inc.
A Grosset & Dunlap Company
360 Park Avenue South
New York, New York 10010

2 4 6 8 0 9 7 5 3 1
Manufactured in the United States of America

THE NOWHERE WEAPON

PROLOGUE

The already-damp carpeting in the lobby absorbed the moisture brought in on the wet shoes of the man who entered the hotel. His brown curly hair was flecked with droplets of rain. He was tall and lean, with a springy stride, restless blue eyes and craggy, angular features. He flapped the lapels of his soiled, off-white trench coat, dislodging the clinging beads of water.

He stepped over to the formica-topped reception desk. The hotel's night manager took a room key and an Air France ticket envelope out of the pigeonholed rack.

"You are leaving, Mr. Randolph?" he asked politely.

The young man's name was not Randolph, but he answered promptly. "Next Wednesday," he lied easily. "I'll be back by the weekend," he lied again. "The room's paid for in advance until then, so please hold it." This last was true. The man addressed as Randolph had made the prepayment so his imminent absence would not be a matter of concern. The ticket he held had been delivered to the hotel from the Paris branch of the American Express Travel Agency. It was for a single seat on tomorrow morning's Air France SST flight to Washington, D.C.

The New Excelsior Hotel was hardly new. The six-story structure had a 1948 cornerstone. It sat on a narrow street four blocks off the Champs Elysee. Through periodic renovation and the retention of a competent, dedicated staff, the hotel had managed to retain much of its original elegance. Its clientele, on the other hand, had become a hybrid crowd of transients, charter airline tour groups, and an operating base for second-string hookers. It was the perfect haven for individuals who wished to maintain a low profile.

The elevators were self-service, and the man in the rain-dampened coat rode alone to his room on the fourth floor. As he walked down the narrow dimly lit hallway, his footsteps squeaked on the asphalt tiles covering the floor. When he pushed the door open, a tiny piece of paper fluttered down next to his foot. Upon seeing the bit of confetti, he entered the room confidently. Inside, he tossed his raincoat on the bed and went into the bathroom to towel dry his wet hair. He looked into the mirror above the washbasin and stared at what he saw: A folded piece of paper was tucked into the frame of the mirror. It had not been there when he had left in mid-afternoon.

He unfolded the paper and read the note.

Fumiere willing to reveal information under certain conditions. Be at Rue Voullaire gate at eleven.

Make certain you are alone.

Excitement surged through him. Even though there was no signature, he recognized the distinctive German penmanship of the handwriting. It belonged to Ernst Rutzmann, a helpful colleague and member of the Deutsches Nachrichdienst whose intelligence headquarters were located in West Berlin. The cryptic message held such promise that the hurried trip back to the United States for the purpose of reporting an impasse in progress might not be necessary after all.

The cautious American looked at his watch. Ten before nine. Time enough to eat in the dining room. The excellent cuisine was one of the advertised attractions of the hotel that lived up to its billing. He ripped the note into small pieces and flushed them down the toilet. Moving to the writing desk next to the bed, he spread out a city map provided by the hotel. Rue Voullaire was a short street on the left bank of the Seine. It formed one boundary of a small park of some sort. He fixed the location in his mind.

On the ground floor, a lounge butted up against the dining room. A bar stretched along one wall. Three working girls and a disinterested man were its customers. The women studied the young man with hopeful, professional curiosity. One with slanted eyes and moist lips turned her head to watch the newcomer climb up on a stool. Her languid stare was much like Collette's when she was in a teasing, lustful mood, he thought. He missed her.

Smiling, he remembered the vivacious, fun-loving French gamine. For nine days she had spent time in his apartment as an off-and-on, dusk-to-dawn companion until he sensed danger and had sent her away for her own good. A week later he was convinced the rooms in the carefully chosen *pension* could be a death trap and left them abruptly.

He was taken away from those disturbing thoughts when the bartender brought his Beefeater's gin and bitters over ice. He drank the first sip slowly, savoring it, then picked up his glass and carried it into the dining room. When the meal arrived, he discovered he was not really hungry. Nerves, he concluded, as he sorted out the diced turnips and ate most of the lamb. He tarried afterward, sipping mediocre coffee, smoking a cigarette, and reading a current copy of *Le Monde* left behind by a previous diner.

At ten o'clock he got up and left. Only the lone male seen earlier at the bar was still there. The young man sauntered up to the reception desk in the lobby, making a show of screening a yawn with his hand. "I'll be turning in early," he told the desk clerk. "If any calls come for me, have the operator take the message. I don't want to be disturbed."

He returned to his room. The bed had been turned down, his packed bag placed on a nearby luggage rack. Nothing else appeared to have been disturbed. He put on his raincoat, then stuck his head out into the hallway. It was empty. Quietly, he walked to the end of the bare corridor. The moisture-swollen window leading out to the fire escape resisted, but made no sound when he forced it open.

The outside temperature had dropped. It was

near freezing. The mist coating the iron structure had turned to rime ice. The footing was treacherous. He went down the fire escape carefully, holding onto the handrail. The courtway behind the hotel was a litter of trash cans, rain-soaked cartons, and a few loose bricks. Motor scooters and mopeds belonging to the hotel staff were chained and padlocked to a parking rack. He ducked low as he went past steam-coated windows lit from the inside. He reached the street, hunched his shoulders and turned up his collar. He walked rapidly west.

After two blocks, he came to a well-lit avenue. City buses, cars, and taxis sped along the street, honking raucously. Their tires flung spray onto the sidewalks. Some shops were open still, but most were dark. He turned the corner onto another major thoroughfare. A frigid, wet wind struck him in the face. He walked slower, then slipped into the shelter of a closed store entryway and lit a cigarette. No one was behind him. The one or two pedestrians that went by him showed no interest. The time was ten past ten.

He left the alcove and started to walk in the opposite direction. Wisps of chill fog spreading beyond the river's banks drifted past. He crossed to the other side of the street and approached a dim neon sign: *Café-Rotisserie-Tabac*. He entered and sat at a small table next to the plate-glass window facing the street. He ordered an expresso and a snifter of brandy. At a quarter to eleven he left.

The fog was patchy. In places, the street lights were only faint halos of brightness. Elsewhere, the sidewalk and street were almost clear. A crowd leaving a cinema flowed around him. He queued up at the curb with others. In moments he was inside a taxi rolling toward the rendezvous with Rutzmann.

The driver dropped him off at the corner of Parc Dutain and Rue Voullaire. He stood in the mist, listening as much as looking. After the sizzle of the departing taxi's wet tires on the pavement faded from hearing, there was no sound. Four and five-story apartment houses lined the left side of the street. Several small European cars were parked along the curb in front. At the end of the block there was a dark sedan, large enough to be a Jaguar or a Bentley. It was too distant from the mid-block street lamp to be identified.

A sign prohibited parking on his side of the street. The curb was free. A wide sidewalk bordered a park or the edge of a cemetery. He couldn't see far in the darkness and the fog. A three-foot high, spiked wrought iron fence enclosed the grassy area. The pointed, sagittal uprights spaced four inches apart dripped beads of moisture. The waist-level row of decorative arrowheads was interrupted further on by an entrance arch containing a closed gate—the Rue Voullaire gate.

He walked forward. After a few steps he saw a bundled figure backed up to the fence. Big enough to be Ernst Rutzmann, its posture was one of casual slumping against the fence. Two more steps and the man approaching the gate knew something was wrong. He ran forward. It was Rutzmann. His eyes were wide open and staring. A frightful grimace covered his face. His top coat was wet with moisture and fresh blood. The crimson stain came from three ghastly wounds. A trio of spiked stakes had pierced his chest from behind when he was lifted and impaled on the fence.

The churn of an engine starter snapped the American's head toward the sound. The fog had lifted for a few yards in that direction. Headlights of the large black sedan came on and probed the darkness. The trapped man looked for sanctuary. He made a sideways, legging leap to clear the fence. The trailing skirt of his trench coat was speared by a picket, holding him fast. The car accelerated with a spin of protesting tires. Looking over his shoulder, he saw the headlights grow larger suddenly, focusing on and blinding him. He ripped off his raincoat using brute strength, tearing buttons and fabric. He struggled out of it. At that instant the fender of the car smashed into his hip.

Intense pain coursed down his leg and shot up into his rib cage. He barely felt the shock of falling to the ground. For a moment he lay without moving. He then tried to raise himself and reach inside his jacket to draw the pistol he carried in a shoulder holster. The movement brought on a sharp, stabbing pain that made him gasp. A thin, singing noise went off in his head. He feared drifting into unconsciousness and fumbled once again to get his gun. That was his last conscious movement.

The black sedan had stopped. A burly man slid out of the seat next to the driver and walked back to the inert form. He bent down and pried open one of the injured man's eyelids. The driver backed the car, making it a screen between the pair and any apartment onlookers.

"*Est-il mort?*" the driver asked.

"*Non.* He is alive."

The driver reached back over the seat and unlatched the rear door. The ashen-faced victim, his soiled clothes pasted with wet leaves from the sidewalk, was hoisted into the back seat. A light went on in the foyer of a building directly opposite. The front door opened. A woman stepped out, restraining an eager poodle on a leash while she opened her umbrella. "Drive away slowly," the burly man cautioned the driver after getting into the car.

Less than a minute after the black sedan had rounded the corner, the woman ran screaming back to her husband that there was a horribly murdered man pinned to the fence across the street.

ONE

The ringing of the telephone forced me to surface from a deep sleep. I opened one eye and squinted at the bedside clock. The dial read 3:14 P.M. After six hours of sleep I was still groggy. I snaked an arm out from under the sheet and groped blindly until my hand struck the receiver. I grunted into the mouthpiece. My tongue was too thick and not yet awake enough to produce intelligible sounds.

"Nick, this is Ginger." Ginger Bateman, a statuesque redhead from Atlanta, is David Hawk's girl Friday whom I always thought would be something special on Saturday nights. "The boss wants you down at headquarters as soon as possible."

I grunted again. This time it came out more like a groan of protest. Ginger hung up without another word. She didn't expect an answer from me. None was needed. Compliance with a request from David Hawk is automatic. And an unscrambled call coming over an open line can only mean that the message is urgent.

A steady rain greeted me when I reached the street. I turned on my headlights and joined the late afternoon traffic moving along Mount Vernon Memorial Highway. The well-traveled road parallels the sluggish Potomac River after skirting Washington National Airport. The massive, gray granite Pentagon Building was barely visible in the rain when I went by. Across the Arlington Memorial Bridge—on the Washington side—water was gushing down the gutters of New Hampshire Avenue as I drove northwest on the midtown thoroughfare.

I parked in the reserved space AXE rents for me in the basement garage of the Dupont Plaza Hotel and went out the fire door exit into the alley. The high walls of buildings on either side provided shelter as I took back alley shortcuts to Massachusetts Avenue. There awnings of chic boutiques and exclusive men's shops kept me dry.

The first alphabetical listing on the directory in the Steadman Building lobby is *Alliance for Peace*. It's located in Suite 514. I always suspected it was a front for something else. The second listing is *Amalgamated Press and Wire Services*. I know that's a phony; it's the cover name for AXE which occupies most of the third floor.

The AXE offices lobby, clearly visible behind handleless, glass, self-opening doors, was empty. It normally is. Very little work goes on in the open. Visitors have to step on a floor-flush pressure plate to activate the automatic doors.

I did, but nothing happened.

THE NOWHERE WEAPON 11

The treadle has a built-in, time-delay mechanism. An eight-second hold enables sophisticated sensing detectors to examine the visitor. A variety of electronic devices concealed in and around the door frame use regular and infrared photography as well as more exotic, invisible probes to obtain and analyze the complete physical and biochemical profile of the individual. The results are fed into a computer for instant comparative tests and retention. No one person knows how detailed the examination is. It's rumored that the procedure comes up with everything from a three-dimensional skull scan to a sperm count.

I waited—and smiled. As I stood there while the high speed security check ran its course, Ginger Bateman came out into the lobby from David Hawk's office. It's not often I get to see Ginger full length and in motion. She's usually seated behind her desk and most of our conversations are over the phone. Seeing her in person is a real treat—she's remarkably pretty and her body is deliciously proportioned.

Finally the doors before me parted and I stepped forward. Ginger's attractive smile was missing. Her lips were pursed and her fine eyebrows were pushed together in a disconcerting frown. "Bad news?" I ventured.

"Must be," she surmised. Her voice, always husky with just a trace of southern accent, came out hushed and thin this time. "I've never seen him so quiet. . . so preoccupied. Go right in. He's waiting for you."

I rapped twice on the heavy oak door, then pushed it open. No lights were on. Hawk sat behind his large executive desk in the semidarkness of the gloomy afternoon. Rain streamed down the windowpane in back of him. It trickled down the glass like a flood of tears. His elbows were dug into the arms of his high-back leather chair while his clenched fists were pushed together to form a V in which his firm chin rested. Hawk didn't look up or speak.

Something was very wrong. The hub-cap size ashtray within reach of his long arm had only one chewed-end cigar stub in it. On a normal day, it would have contained a half dozen butts by this time. Hawk's eyes were open, but not registering my presence; he was deep in thought.

I cleared my throat politely.

Hawk didn't alter his pose. "Sorry, Nick," his normally clear, resonant voice mumbled. "Have a seat."

Yes, something *was* wrong. Hawk seldom apologized. He had few reasons to, so when he did, it was definitely out of character. The prolonged silence was another indication that he was troubled. As director and operations chief of AXE, the elite, clandestine intelligence organization that has no published charter, David Hawk maintains a fast pace. He manipulates the obscure, worldwide actions of AXE and its unique agent staff with deft and respected expertise.

Whatever Hawk had on his mind, it obviously would involve my talents when he got around to laying it out.

I sat down. Hawk's shaded profile was indistinct but nevertheless stony. I wondered why he had summoned me if he was unsure of what he wanted to discuss. It had to be serious. His reticence made me uncomfortable.

Hawk raised his eyes momentarily to glance up at the wall clock anchored over his office door. It had five hands. Two of them told me it was now 4:34 here in Washington. The other three hour hands indicated local times in London, Tokyo, and Moscow. "We have to wait for a phone call," he said flatly, then lapsed into silence again. The incoming message must be an extraordinary one to keep Hawk so much on edge.

I jumped when the telephone rang. The impact of the very ordinary sound told me how tensed-up the enforced silence had made me. Hawk broke his pose to reach sideways to pick up the receiver. "Yes, sir?" The greeting was most respectful. To my knowledge there is only one person in all of Washington whom Hawk addresses as 'sir.' It was a one-sided conversation. During its three-minute duration, Hawk responded with "yes, sir" four times. After the fourth one, he hung up.

The long wait was over. Hawk uncapped the humidor on his desk and drew out one of his cheap cigars. "Smoke if you like," he invited in a voice forced up through a dry throat.

I lit a gold-tipped, filter cigarette made with my private, custom-blended tobacco. My initials, N.C., were imprinted in gold on the slim cylinder. Hawk's typical reaction is to look down his impressive aquiline nose at what he considers an affectation. Today he merely swiveled his chair around to get up and stand with his back to me. He stared out through the rain-drenched window as he fired up his cigar. He watched traffic weaving in and around busy Dupont Circle like rubber-bumpered dodge 'em cars in an amusement park.

Hawk began puffing nervously on his cigar. A foul-smelling smoke screen welled up between us. I knew he was mulling over the comments and instructions he'd received from the White House. When he turned around, snapped on his desk lamp, and seated himself again, I gave him my full attention.

His first words were underlined by a sustained rumble of thunder overhead. "One of our people seems to have disappeared. In Paris." It came out as a bland, matter-of-fact statement. Because he said it calmly and sans emotion, it sounded all the more sinister to me.

A dozen possibilities raced through my mind. AXE missions generally involve some danger. They are always unique—largely due to very unorthodox techniques generally employed, especially by those granted an "N" classification like myself. It's never been revealed to me how many "N" operatives AXE has or who my predecessors are...or were. When the disappearance of an agent creates such a stir that the president takes a personal interest in the matter, the situation must be badly off track.

"It's a puzzler, Nick," Hawk said softly. "Our man, going by the name of Randolph, was due back from Paris two days ago. He was given a simple courier job, but one of extreme importance. The material he was to pick up and bring with him is absolutely vital to secret research the Defense Department is conducting on an advanced weapons system. The data Randolph was expected to deliver is a discovery made—and kept secret—by Volmer Ulrich, an outstanding Eastern European electrochemist. Ulrich was ... shall we say ... enticed to come over to our side, bringing with him details of his spectacular technological breakthrough. It's expected to revolutionize current concepts of military tactics."

"Perhaps Randolph hit a snag and is keeping a low profile for the time being," I suggested.

"There were ways for him to advise us of any delays," Hawk snapped. "He shouldn't have run into any trouble. The danger element was relatively low. At last contact, everything was running smoothly. Too smoothly, perhaps. The Ulrich data was all but in our hands; Randolph had already booked a flight from Orly to Dulles International. Everything was set, then—poof! He vanished without a trace. I'll have to admit that, at this point, I'm as concerned as I am puzzled."

His teeth gnawed and bit down hard on his smoldering cigar. That told me that he was probably angry at himself for underestimating problems Randolph could have encountered. I guessed he was under severe pressure because the poor slob in Paris had botched it.

"I've no other choice, Nick. Someone has to move in quickly in case Randolph has gotten in over his head."

"I just came back from a rough assignment, sir," I reminded him.

"I know," he replied. It was an automatic response with no thanks in it. But I knew better than to argue. "I'm asking you to go over and finish the job. Find where it's been bobbled and tie up any loose ends that have come unravelled. You can start with or without locating Randolph—that's up to you. The information he was after is your first priority. Get it and get it back here." Hawk snatched the half-smoked cigar from his mouth and broke its neck grinding out the lighted end in his ashtray.

I waited for Hawk to continue; there had to be more to go on. Finally he pulled a folder from the center drawer of his desk and handed it to me. It contained a single sheet of paper with a 5x7 head-and-shoulder photograph of passport quality pasted in its center. The subject was a young, sandy-haired man with an Ivy League look about him.

"Good-looking lad," Hawk commented. "He was a State Department employee based in Paris until we recruited him three weeks ago for this job. He was right for it. For more than a year he was the chief courier transporting classified material between Paris and Bonn."

"He was being used for the first time?" I asked incredulously.

"It was a simple, straightforward bit of business." Hawk sounded defensive.

"Any chance he discovered what he was carrying in his hot little hands and decided to sell it back to the other side?"

"Not likely," Hawk said sharply. "Randolph was as straight as a laser beam. He was too charged up with initial loyalty and wanting to prove himself to consider turning. Besides, we aren't sure he actually got his hands on it. If he had, and was intercepted, we would have detected some reaction from the other side by now."

"How was Randolph to make the pick-up?"

"The usual way . . . through a drop established to hold it until it was safe for Randolph to go there."

"Who was supposed to pass the drop location to Randolph?"

"The lead was coming out of West Germany through a Nachrichtendienst network in France. We don't know who the agent was. Randolph was told not to pass along the names of any contacts. We didn't want the French government to stumble across the fact that we had an active connection with the Germans in Paris. Our relations with the French are precarious at best right now. Which is why I've had to coordinate matters directly with the Oval office. So whatever you do, play it cool so there won't be any diplomatic repercussions."

I knew what he meant. No messiness. No killing. Why was he telling me something that had been drilled into me time and again? For the first time, Hawk was taking great pains to avoid something.

"Sounds ominous," I said.

"Ernst Rutzmann was murdered in Paris the same day Randolph sent us word that he was coming back," Hawk said with no trace of emotion. "It could be pure coincidence. We're trying to get a reading from Bonn now."

"If Rutzmann was the contact," I offered, "Randolph could be running for his life. If so, and I find myself faced with nothing but dead ends, I might have to bend the rules a little."

Hawk stood up. His move signalled that he had told me everything I could expect to hear. It wasn't near enough. I imagined that Randolph felt the same after he had signed up. If he did, we had something in common: a feeling of being very much alone.

As I got to my feet, Hawk stuck out his hand. I took it. His grip was firm, extra tight. He hung on longer than usual. "A security officer from our embassy in Paris will meet you and fill you in on what they know. Right now that's little more than the location of Randolph's apartment on the left bank of the Seine in Montparnasse." He drew a breath, then pursed his lips. His words, "Good Luck," came out through nearly-clenched teeth.

Ginger Bateman was waiting for me outside of Hawk's door. She handed me a large bulging envelope. "Passport, first-class Pan Am ticket, and enough francs to buy the Eiffel Tower from a street vendor." Her smile was forced. Her large brown eyes weren't laughing. "You're on Flight 187 leaving Dulles International at 8:48 tonight."

For a moment, we both had hold of the envelope. Ginger used it to pull herself toward me. By standing on tiptoe, she was able to reach my cheek to plant a kiss on it. As I turned away to leave, she called out "Hurry back" in a soft voice. Then she spun around abruptly and hurried away.

It was as close to a tearful goodbye as I'd ever gotten. I only hoped my leaving wouldn't turn out to be a permanent absence.

I drove to my Arlington, Virginia high-rise apartment in the continuing downpour. It had been Indian-summer muggy and raining steadily for three days. The weather in Paris couldn't be any worse.

I felt better as soon as I reached the air-conditioned interior of the building. My mood improved with each muffled step along the thick pile carpeting leading to my apartment. Although I spent far too little time in it, my suite was well-furnished and cozy. The door was jerked open before my key had turned in the lock.

Then I remembered that Malua was probably still there.

"Nick!" She greeted me at the door with a freshly-made drink and a warm, moist kiss. "I took some steaks out of your freezer so we won't have to go out for dinner in this weather," she beamed.

Her growing affection was reaching a dangerously possessive level. "I hope you didn't take seriously any promises I made to you about this weekend," I told her. I wanted Malua to understand that our friendship was no more committing on my part than sharing an occasional romp.

Malua, a gorgeous, full-blooded Hawaiian lass, laughed with exotic, deep-throated tones that reminded me of the surf pounding the beach at Keaau. "Nick, honey, I'll never be a threat to your bachelorhood, but I challenge your stamina." She stretched out both arms and rested her wrists on my shoulders. The casual action caused the deep cleavage of her low-cut dress to gape open. The luscious, braless curves of her full, tawny-skinned breasts were as stimulating as the first warm sip of the drink she had given me.

She surged forward. The entire length of her body pressed against mine. We fit together tightly from chest to knee, The heady scent of the plumeria blossom tucked into her shining black hair assailed my nostrils. She laid her lips against my ear and whispered huskily, "What would you like for an hors d'oeuvre?"

The innuendo was unmistakable. The appetizer she had in mind had nothing to do with canapes.

I detached myself from her and backed away, dropping into my favorite upholstered chair. Malua pursued me, plopping herself down on my lap. She wiggled her bottom in a pretense of getting settled properly. It brought about a perfectly natural and predictable response from me. I put aside my drink. My hands gently smoothed over the contours of her lush body. I bent my head down so my lips could reach the depression between her warm breasts. "Let's skip the food for now," I muttered into soft flesh.

I wasn't hungry, really . . . except for her. Still, I had the presence of mind to give priority to having my bag packed so I would have it with me when I caught that night flight. Malua frowned with surprise when I stood up summarily and nearly tumbled her from my lap.

When Malua heard that I had to leave shortly, she seemed determined to see that I got a proper, memorable sendoff. She kept teasing me with active hands and pushing herself against me while I put things into my travel-scuffed two-suiter bag.

I finally gave up. The zipper down the back of her emerald-green dress slithered open easily. Malua stepped back and shrugged her shoulders. The soft fabric cascaded off her slender body. She stood in front of me needle-naked, breathtakingly beautiful, and smiling. She wore the merest whisp of translucent bikini panties.

I sprinkled her bare shoulder with kisses as we moved to the bed. Our lovemaking was uninhibited, furious, and demanding. We shared a deep-felt, lingering togetherness that would be a long-remembered goodbye. Reluctantly I dragged myself away.

While showering, my mind reverted back to what Hawk had said about the job he needed done in Paris. The variations that could have brought about Randolph's sudden disappearance were unsettling.

The bothersome question was whether Randolph had his hands on the all-important material before he dropped from sight. If that was the case, the situation was clouded with a very negative ingredient. If he had been trailed and snatched—kidnapped while still empty-handed—he could be undergoing horrible torture. I didn't think he'd be able to hold out long before he screamed out some answers; his photograph didn't reflect strength in the physical resistance department.

On the brighter side, Randolph could simply have missed a contact and was reluctant to admit failure. There was always the chance of a young, unwary agent stumbling badly and blowing his cover. I couldn't hold onto that upbeat assumption. It was replaced immediately with the possibility that someone had stumbled onto Randolph and had blown him away. One other consideration crossed my mind. A captured Randolph could be used as a decoy to lure bigger and more useful game into a well-planned snare. An icy shiver coursed down my back as I left the shower stall. I felt far from comfortable about what I was getting into as I toweled myself.

Malua was asleep and breathing with a contented, kittenlike purr when I bent down and kissed her ear.

The last things I packed in my suitcase were the trio of weapons that go everywhere with me. Hawk had said nothing about being armed; that was my own judgement. My decisions are generally based on cold logic, but sometimes I follow hunches. On more than one occasion I've ended up alive because I did. In this instance, the facts were so sketchy that I let instinct guide me. An eerie, gnawing feeling of doubt made the choice easy.

TWO

Not long after the opening of the new Charles de Gaulle airport on the northwestern outskirts of Paris, Orly Field began to deteriorate. At one time Orly was among the ten busiest airports in the world. Now it was definitely second-rate in all categories. Pan Am continued to use it for some flights. I still prefer it. Compared to de Gaulle, Orly is half the distance away from the center of Paris and one can process through French customs in half the time.

Customs clearance was not a concern this trip. Hawk's arrangement to have me met by an American embassy official with diplomatic status would enable me to bypass much of the bureaucratic maze other arriving foreigners have to endure. I spotted him at once. To me, the cut of American tailoring stands out against a background of European-styled clothes. The man wore his custom-fitted business suit well. He had the build for it. He was close to six feet in height with wide shoulders and a narrow waist. The hand he put out to shake mine and to take my passport from me had blunt, manicured fingernails. "I'm Ralph Springer," the young man announced. A large-toothed grin under a blocky brown mustache gave his broad, boyish face a Teddy Roosevelt appearance when he smiled.

His voice was a disappointment. Despite a big frame and thick neck, his speech was high-pitched and came out like he was practicing diction lessons. He was much younger than I first thought. I sensed this because, after his first hearty greeting, he seemed uncertain as to how to proceed. Aggressiveness was not one of his obvious traits. He acted as though this was his first try at being a red tape expeditor. It occurred to me that Springer, no doubt the most junior member of the State Department security staff, was the only one the embassy cared to spare. The inference did little to inflate my ego.

Under my critical gaze, Springer moved into action. His inertia overcome, Springer was efficient enough in getting me through the French port of entry. Having succeeded with far less trouble than he expected, his shy attitude changed. He assumed that he was entitled to take charge. He motioned for me to take my bag which the customs inspector shoved across the counter, then started to walk away. He expected me to follow him.

I didn't.

When he noticed that I was not walking beside him, Springer stopped and looked back over his shoulder. Our eyes met. "Is something wrong?" he tossed at me. The sharp inflection he used made the question sound as though he was demanding an answer instead of asking for one. I resented his tone.

"Where are we going?" I worked to keep my voice level.

Springer gestured with a casual wave of his hand. "An official sedan with a driver is parked out in front. My instructions were to provide you with any reasonable assistance. I thought—"

"Let's take a look," I agreed.

Springer responded with a questioning knitting of his eyebrows, then proceeded across the terazzo-floored terminal lobby. As we neared the exit doors, I grabbed Springer's muscle-packed arm. I drew him to one side. Together we looked out through the massive glass walls of the building to see the street. The clearly-marked U.S. government vehicle was starkly conspicuous in the bright morning sunshine. It stood alone at curbside under a large sign that prohibited parking. A Parisian gendarme, wearing a thigh-length cape and swinging a white-painted nightstick idly, was engaged in conversation with the embassy driver.

"I really don't understand your behavior, Mr. Carter." Springer again phrased his words with condescending impatience.

His officious manner was becoming increasingly difficult to bear. "Humor me," I said through clenched teeth.

Springer wisely fell silent and stood by as I scanned the area before us. His curiosity finally got the best of him. "Do you see something out there that—"

Right then I knew that some phases of Springer's

security training had been neglected. "I see a French cop talking to your driver," I cut in. "Like police all over the world, he's probably underpaid. That makes him corruptible. So he earns a little on the side to keep his eyes and ears open. A lot of people are interested in who leaves or arrives in Paris . . . especially foreigners who rate official transportation. Whether that gendarme is on the take or not, as a cop he's obligated to inform *la Sûreté* anything he observes that is out of the ordinary."

As I explained, Springer's head began to nod with understanding. When he turned to face me, I noticed a change in his expression. Respect flickered from his deep-set eyes. "I guess I should have had the car wait someplace else."

"Never mind that now. Are you authorized to drive an official sedan?"

"Yes. Why?"

"Go out and tell your chauffeur—making sure that gendarme overhears you—that I wasn't on the plane. Don't use any names. Say that the party you were to meet was delayed and will be on an Air Canada flight due to arrive in two hours. Tell your driver that you'll take over from him and wait with the car. Give him the rest of the morning off. Tell him to take the Metro back to town and report in at the embassy motor pool after lunch. Give him a few francs . . . enough for a bread, cheese and wine lunch even if he brought a brown bag with him."

"That's highly irregular." Springer's protest was a mild one.

"That's the way I do things. I thought you were told to cooperate."

"I might have some explaining to do," he considered.

"About dismissing the driver or hampering my assignment?" I asked pointedly.

"I'll get on it," he conceded. "I suppose you'll want a rental car for your own use?"

"No. That's another sure-fire way to advertise you're a new kid in town. It looks like we're stuck with each other. Besides, I need you. Take the embassy car into the public parking lot. Stay with it. Wait ten minutes, then bail yourself out. You'll find me, bag in hand, walking alongside the exit road that connects with Route A-6 leading to the city. On the way in you can tell me what you know about the missing man." I turned away and started in the direction of the rest rooms.

Springer appeared to pull off the role of disappointed welcomer with ease. I watched his performance, standing well back from the thick glass walls. The gendarme retreated a step to allow Springer to reach the driver's window. Whether through curiosity or courtesy, the policeman remained beside the car. The chauffeur relinquished his position to Springer without argument. The cop presented a polite, bowed-head, two finger salute as Springer drove off in the sedan. No words passed between the displaced driver and the polite gendarme as they went their separate ways.

The policeman stepped out into the traffic lane and began urging automobiles to keep moving. He crossed to the opposite curb where he used his nightstick to wave into motion a parked Fiat stationwagon. The next automobile in line was a Citroën sedan. The gendarme exchanged a few words with its apparently argumentative driver before it, too, moved on. Both cars fell in line behind Springer who was now signalling for a turn into the parking lot.

I watched the street and the patrolling cop for a full minute. Then I continued to the rest room carrying my two suiter. By applying the leverage of his diplomatic immunity, Springer had gotten my luggage cleared without its being opened or subjected to the usual declaration of contents. That kind of help was invaluable to me.

The francs spent for the privacy of a pay toilet was a typical expense account item. Inside the cubicle, I removed my jacket and hung it on the hook on the back of the locked door. I opened my bag and took out the soft chamois holster that held Wilhelmina, a deadly 9mm Luger automatic. I strapped the holster around my chest so the weapon fitted snugly under my left armpit. I've become so accustomed to it being there that I feel undressed without it.

Next I strapped a flat, leather scabbard holding a modified World War II British commando knife to my right forearm. It's a lethal weapon in practiced hands. Mine has its tapered blade shortened to four inches. A four-inch length is more than enough; both heart and jugular vein are buried less than three inches inside a man's body. The cutdown blade altered the knife's original perfect balance, but didn't hinder my ability to place the gnarled handle instantly in my fingers by a supinating flip of my wrist.

The most sophisticated weapon of my three-part arsenal is Pierre, a small spherical bomb with the killing power of a supercharged hand grenade. It has a thumb-actuated, multiple-setting fuse control that gives it great versatility. Compact and ping-pong ball size, Pierre is carried concealed between my legs. It nestles tightly in my crotch, almost like a third testicle.

After pulling up and belting my trousers, I rolled down my loose-cuffed shirt sleeve and put on my jacket. I felt much more confident when I left the rest room.

Springer did a very smooth job of picking me up. He had the passenger door unlatched and partly open as he slowed the sedan alongside. I quickened my steps. I shoved my suitcase ahead of me into the front seat, then swung aboard like a railroad yard switchman hopping a rolling boxcar. The flow of exiting traffic was impeded only for a moment.

"Well done," I said sincerely. I felt I had to say something to get a fresh start at building rapport. Springer merely glanced at me to acknowledge my brief compliment. He wasn't quite ready to be won over. After fitting the car into the stream of traffic hurtling along Route A-6, he drove with eyes straight ahead, jaw fixed. He kept to the right-hand side, leaving the other two lanes to the French commuters who drove as if each was tormented by an impelling death wish. "Tell me what you know about the man who went by the name of Randolph," I said encouragingly.

"I really didn't know him," Springer confessed. "I saw him around the embassy once or twice, but that was some time ago. I was told he was a courier, but lately I started thinking he was a field man for the Central Intelligence Agency. That was after he became less evident. He was working under some kind of cover ... or at least that's the impression I got."

"You must have based that conclusion on more than a notion," I remarked.

"Well, that's true," he admitted. "I knew he was up to something when my chief issued a work order to make a sweep of the apartment he occupied. We did it while he was off somewhere."

So Springer's expertise was in communications. "When did you look around his place?"

"Just two weeks ago yesterday."

That figured. Hawk said that Randolph had been recruited three weeks ago. "Did you find anything?"

"The place was clean. Electronically speaking," he added. "His girl friend wasn't much of a housekeeper."

"He had a live-in companion?"

"Could have had a dozen girls in and out of there. He was a handsome stud, all right."

A road sign flashed by. Midtown Paris was fourteen kilometers ahead. I had been sitting with my feet propped up on the two-suiter and my legs were beginning to cramp. Springer ducked as I lifted the bag over the back of the front seat. While twisted around, I glanced out through the rear window.

Cars were packed three abreast on the road. Those in the two outer lanes were travelling at breakneck speed. Immediately behind us was a black Citroën. If it was the same one I had seen at the Orly terminal, the lone driver had been joined by two other men since the gendarme had asked him to move.

I turned around and faced forward. By adjusting the rear-view mirror properly, I could keep my eye on the following car. It paced us for a quarter of a mile before it swung out and went around. The men inside looked neither to the left or right. A trio of glum-faced, silent businessmen totally bored with each other and the daily routine of sharing a ride to work. I lost sight of the car as other passing vehicles formed a screen between us. Farther on I noticed another black Citroën parked on the shoulder of the highway. It appeared empty. It could have been standing there for hours. I kept my illusory thought to myself, discounting my fleeting concern as super-caution accentuated by jet lag. There was no point in alarming Springer.

I revived our previous conversation. My visual attention, however, was focused on the roadway behind us. "So you won the toss and were picked to meet me on the basis that you'd been to Randolph's apartment once before."

"Something like that," Springer replied. "I also have to report to my boss later so he can notify yours over the embassy's secure communication link to Washington that you got here and are on the job."

"That's routine," I agreed. We had reached the Montrouge turnoff. "I know my way around this part of the city. All I really need from you now is the address."

Springer kept driving. "I hope you don't think me obstinate, Mr. Carter. I'm just following orders. I was told to see to it that you were personally accompanied to your final destination. It's not much farther."

I took another long look behind as Springer veered onto the off ramp. A large, tractor-trailer was following our route, blocking my vision. If a car was trailing us, it had the decided advantage of ample concealment.

THREE

Springer got behind a No. 9 bus on Boulevard Raspail and trailed it to Boulevard de Montparnasse. The prominence of Rodin's famous statue of Honoré de Balzac at the intersection has been greatly diminished since the erection of a towering, fifty-eight-story ferro-concrete office building in the background.

I was marveling at the marked contrast when Springer made a hard right turn.

The unique section of Montparnasse retains much of its Bohemian character. At the turn of the century it became the haven for students, intellectuals, and political firebrands. It has changed little since then. The area still has its share of students. Many of them live in its small hotels. They buy books in its musty old bookstores and eat in its crowded *bistros* that spread cooking odors through its twisting, ancient streets. Of the twelve thousand serious artists and art students in Paris, at least half live, study, or work in Montparnasse. Art shops and galleries line the wide boulevards. Some of the side streets have atmosphere, but most are narrow and canyonlike. Old, multi-storied buildings hold back the sunshine except at midday.

Springer stopped along the curb in front of one. He had wound about and backtracked slightly before turning off Rue Notre Dame de Champs into Rue Laverrier. The corroded metal numbers on a plaque next to the door read 247. "This is it," he announced.

I got out and stood on the sidewalk. The building was a narrow, six-story structure. Its entrance was squeezed between a pleasant, yeasty-smelling bakery shop and a leather goods store. The street-level doors led into a tile-floored lobby. At the far end was an elevator which brought to mind an oversized bird cage. The shaft was enclosed by thin, paint-peeling, plastered walls. Short flights of stairs boxing in the shaft as it rose provided an alternate means of reaching the upper floors.

I preceded Springer into the small cab. The two of us almost filled it. "It's supposed to hold four people," Springer said skeptically. The warning was printed on a placard mounted above a vertical row of five floor-selector buttons. He pressed the top one. A gear wheel on the cab roof turned. The cables jerked, and the bird cage rose. We could have walked up the stairs faster.

A telephone began ringing above us as we went by the third floor. "It's his!" Springer exclaimed when he heard it again as we passed the fourth floor. It was still ringing when we left the elevator on the fifth.

Springer had a key. He thrust it into the keyhole as the bell inside pealed again. He dashed inside and lifted the receiver. "Damn!" he swore explosively. "They hung up!"

Days-old stale air filled the apartment. I went to the window overlooking the street. Rue Laverrier was quiet and normal from all appearances. It took a full minute of watching for me to reach that conclusion. Then I opened the window and let in some fresh air.

The apartment was compact and efficient. It had two principle rooms: a small sitting room with a cooking alcove attached, and a bedroom with tiny, adjoining shower-equipped bath. A cursory examination of the bedroom wardrobe and medicine chest contents told me that Randolph had left hurriedly. A look into the small refrigerator confirmed that his departure had occurred some time ago.

"You'll want to take a look at this, Mr. Carter," Springer called out to me. He was standing beside a marble-topped chiffonier looking at some scraps of paper.

I crossed the room, but ignored Springer. My attention was drawn to a framed, full-length color photograph of a striking blonde, pixie-faced girl. It was a blow-up of a snapshot taken at a beach. The subject was all but nude; her costume was a string bikini. It was hard to guess her age—more than a child, but perhaps not yet a woman. Her bold, round eyes carried the knowing look of maturity ... widespaced and challenging above a provacative, full-lipped smile. She was all woman except in one vital department. Nature had cheated her. She was pitifully flat chested. The deficiency was amply offset by long, gracefully-shaped legs and a saucy derriere.

"I'll bet she's really something!" Springer

beamed, noting that my attention had been diverted to the photograph. I thought to myself: We've finally found something we can agree upon.

"What'd you find?"

"Some odds and ends that might tell you something about how he lived."

There was a book of twenty Metro tickets; eight had been used. A doubled-over envelope from a dry cleaning establishment on Rue Tournefort contained a claim check. Two outdated balcony seat tickets for an orchestra concert at the Palais de Chaillot were for a performance given three weeks ago. I was making a mental note of a garage address on a rent receipt for automobile storage when the telephone rang again.

Springer moved fast. His hand was already around the receiver when I jammed mine down on top of it. "Let it ring," I said, peeling his fingers loose. He glowered at me momentarily, then stepped back.

After the third ring, I answered. "Allo?" I speak French like a direct descendant of Napolean. It's my best second language, but this time I intentionally made it sound as if my mouth was stuffed with food.

I barely heard the voice on the other end. The words were in English, spoken precisely as if rehearsed. "The suit to be pressed for Randolph is ready. Bring the claim check."

For a moment I was speechless. I covered my hesitation with a muffled cough. I wanted to hear the voice again. "Did you call just a few minutes ago?" I asked, speaking in soft, slow-paced English.

After a pause: "Yes. No one answered." The

guarded reply carried a marked French accent.

No dry cleaner anywhere in the world makes repeated phone calls to a customer to tell him his clothes can be picked up. Not if the claim check is sent to him through the mail. It was risky to prolong a conversation which had begun with a message that had nothing to do with valet service. I curbed the temptation to verify my conclusion, mumbled a simple "thank you" and hung up.

"Who was that?"

"The dry cleaner," I said, watching for Springer's reaction. "I have to leave. First, I'm going to take a shower and get out of these clothes." I tossed my wrinkled, travel-weary jacket onto the bed. Springer's eyes widened respectfully when he saw my shoulder-holstered gun. "Would you mind going down to the car and bringing up my bag? Then you needn't stick around. But thanks for all your help." I called out those last words from inside the bathroom. I turned the shower on full force to discourage an answer.

I wasted little time refreshing myself. When I turned off the shower, I could hear Springer talking on the telephone. My two-suiter lay on the bed. I could hear some of Springer's conversation coming around the corner as I dressed. From Springer's businesslike language, I gathered that the Kathy he spoke to was an embassy employee. I didn't bother to eavesdrop. As far as I was concerned, our temporary relationship had come to a conclusive end. I finished dressing before he completed his call. He was still talking when I walked past him and closed the apartment door behind me.

The elevator was down at street level. I used the

stairs to save time. The elevator started up when I was halfway down. As soon as I reached the street I crossed it. Shadows inside a doorway gave me cover while I watched the entrance to No. 247.

Springer came out of it at a run. He stopped at the curb and looked up and down the street anxiously. Then he circled the sedan to reach the driver's door. He stood there and repeated his search of the street. His head was turned away when I slipped up behind him.

"Looking for me?"

"Ah . . . er . . . no, sir," Springer stammered. He was a lousy liar.

"Let's stop bugging each other," I flared. "I don't care what instructions you just got over the phone. Back off! You'll only get underfoot and screw up my act. I've gotten all the help from you that I need. This is where we split." I reached around him and yanked open the car door. My other hand on his arm urged him toward the driver's seat.

Springer's temper erupted. He shoved me away with more spirit and strength than I figured him to have. I reeled back a step to regain my balance. then I consciously surged forward, ramming Springer up against the side of the sedan. His breath whooshed out of his lungs. He gasped hoarsely. His hands came up in a gesture of surrender. "There's no need to act like street ruffians," he wheezed. "If you insist going on your own, understand it's under protest on my part."

"Blame me," I snorted. "You mean well. When the time comes I'll ask for help. I don't need it now. If I ever do, you'll be the first to know."

Springer dropped his half-raised hands. He did it slowly.

A truce was in effect.

He was getting into the driver's seat as I walked toward the corner where I could hail a taxi. I looked back once. Springer was getting out of the car again. I saw him go into the apartment house. The closest telephone was there.

The interior of the dry cleaning shop was steamy warm. It also smelled strongly of naphtha. The smiling, elderly man behind the counter had a crease-etched face and bad teeth. He was farsighted, too. He held the claim check within three inches of his nose to identify it.

His smile faded. He looked me over carefully. He pointed behind me with a gnarled, arthritic finger. "Over there. Across the street. Take it to Fumiere. He's the one you want." His accent-laced English sounded much like that I had heard on the telephone. He thrust the claim check into my hand. His crooked finger waved an unmistakable, impatient message to leave at once.

The "treasure hunt" aspect was mystifying. I looked upon it as an annoying runaround. Whatever maze Randolph had constructed to protect his back seemed more like a child's game than serious business.

A bell tinkled over my head when I went through Fumiere's shop door. It was a single, large, noisy room. His business was selling and repairing watches and clocks. There must have been forty loud-ticking, pendulum-swinging grandfather clocks standing like sentinels against the side walls. Six feet inside the door, two glass display cases with a customer counter between them formed a barrier. Behind it, in a low-walled cubicle, a hunched-over man was working at a watchmaker's bench. A green eye shade fitted over his large head. Wisps of stringy, gray hair hung down over his ears. His shoulders and torso were thick, layered with both fat and muscle.

He removed a jeweler's loupe from his eye, then turned to look in my direction. He had a full, moonlike face with small, deep-set eyes. They glared at me coldly, as if any interruption of his work was unwelcome. He set aside the watch he was working on gently. He slid back from the workbench without rising. It was not until he had cleared the low enclosure surrounding his workspace that I was aware he was a cripple. His tremendous arms rolled the wheelchair containing his big torso and skinny, useless legs with ease.

I laid the claim check on the counter where he could see it. He barely glanced at it before locking onto my face with his steely eyes.

"You've got the wrong shop, monsieur." His gruff, rolling French was as deep as one would expect his huge chest to produce. The way he phrased his words made what he said sound more like a question than a curt dismissal.

"I was sent here from across the street," I answered in his native tongue.

Fumiere's sparse eyebrows lifted a millimeter or two. "There's no name on this claim check." Again his tone implied an answer was expected.

"It's Randolph," I responded. "I was told the

items I wanted were ready to be picked up." I suddenly felt I might have acted impulsively. I should have put off following the claim check lead until I had advised Hawk of the development. He may have turned up other useful information he hoped to obtain. It was too late to backtrack now.

Fumiere studied me for a long moment. "How did you come here?" he asked finally.

"By taxi."

"*Sacre Dieu!*" he gagged. "You should have used the Metro. Taxi drivers can be bribed." He wasn't telling me anything new. I had to curb a smile. By openly expressing his fears, Fumiere had told me I had been accepted.

"Watch the street!" he ordered, then whirled his wheelchair around decisively. He propelled himself back to his partially-concealed cubicle.

I placed myself next to the street door. The large glass window that was the shop's front wall needed washing. Through it, I could see half a block in either direction. The street looked normal. Near the corner, a store clerk was cranking down a striped awning to shade the front of his shop.

Behind me, I heard the sound of a telephone being dialed. A moment later, Fumiere began talking. His voice was low-pitched, his words muffled. Once during the conversation the word "money" was mentioned. I glanced over my shoulder. Fumiere was doodling on a calendar pad before him as he talked. He sensed I was watching him. I avoided the hard look he shot back by returning my attention to the street.

Following more hushed discussion, I heard the telephone being replaced. "*Alors!*" Fumiere called out. "We can now proceed."

"There was a question about money?" I tossed over my shoulder.

"That is finished," his nearby voiced proclaimed.

I spun around. The invalid had wheeled his rubber-tired chair noiselessly to reposition himself up against the customer counter. His arms were hanging down at his sides, his hands out of sight.

"So now you have something to give me!" I proposed.

His reply was disappointing. "A time and a place," he answered. As he spoke, his eyes shifted from mine to look out into the street. "Tonight at precisely ten o'clock," Fumiere continued. "Number 78 Rue Hendrix. Near Place de la Dujon."

His voice slowed as he spoke.

Something he was thinking—or seeing—was getting his full attention.

FOUR

The instructions Fumiere relayed to me sounded legitimate, but I've learned to be leery of secondhand telephoned information passed to me by someone of short acquaintance. The peculiar look on Fumiere's face as he sat hunched there in his wheelchair was far from reassuring. His features were tense. I felt a positive premonition of danger when his eyes widened.

I whirled around to see what had attracted his gaze. It was not so much the previously seen black Citroën sedan pulling away from a parking space midway down the block that drove me into action; it was those pipelike objects thrust out of the car's windows. All were pointed in my direction.

Fumiere had triggered the trap with his guarded phone call. The message he had given me was pure bullshit.

I spun back around to deal with him first. I dropped into a crouch as I turned.

During that blurred movement, I was drawing

out Wilhelmina and flicking off the safety. While still in motion and far from actually facing Fumiere—already a dead man in my mind—I saw that he had anticipated my reaction. A sawed-off, double-barreled shotgun in his hands was leveled and about to be fired. The range was less than six feet.

The blast in my face was deafening. It drowned out the sound of shattering shop window glass as the charge whistled past my head.

By the time I was set, with Wilhelmina lined up with Fumiere's heart, I realized he couldn't have missed me at that distance. I wasn't the target. The car moving along the street was his target. Fumiere was not my enemy; he was an ally.

I whipped around again just as the weapons from the now fast-moving car opened fire. Bullets chewed at the door frame, striking only inches above my head. Wood splinters sprinkled down on me. The plate glass framed in the ship door disintegrated into a thousand pieces. Sharp, biting slivers of razor-edged glass showered over me.

I snapped off two quick shots. One of them found its mark. The car, now passing by at full getaway speed, swerved wildly. The two automatic weapons it carried kept up a steady hail of lead, hosing the entire shop interior with inaccurate but death-dealing fire. I hugged the floor, waiting for the drumming explosions to cease.

They stopped suddenly, cut off abruptly by a tremendous crash. I looked up. The racing Citroën, guided by the dead hands of the driver who had one of Wilhelmina's bullets buried in his brain, had leaped the curb and rammed into the common wall between the dry cleaning shop and the wine merchant's store next to it. Bottles displayed behind the smashed street-front window flew about like hard-hit ten pins. Wine and spirits gushed over the sidewalk. Burgundy and claret flowing over the sidewalk looked like free-running blood. The pungent odor of raw alcohol permeated the air.

The inert automobile was partly hidden in a mist, shrouded in steam issuing from burst pipes in the dry cleaning shop. The wall crumbling impact had toppled its gas-fired water heater. An angry, open flame spurted from the broken gas line at its base. The unleashed jet of fire shot out toward the spreading pool of gasoline forming under the wrecked sedan's fuel tank.

Before I could duck, a blast of blinding, heated air struck me. A canopy of vivid orange flame enveloped the disabled car. I could see a pair of men inside working at the car doors in an effort to get out. The front door on the passenger's side was jammed tight. The man trapped behind it was grim-faced. His stern, dark features—bisected by a wide, heavy mustache—showed intense concentration, but no fear. With remarkable coolness, he quickly turned the butt of his weapon into a sledge. Using powerful strokes, he battered a hole in the glass of the windshield to create an exit. It was his only chance. As the determined man squirmed out onto the hood of the car, I could see that his enormous shoulders were far too wide to permit him to wriggle out through the side door window.

His struggling companion in the back seat finally got the rear door open. The frantic man piled out of the fiercely burning automobile and tumbled into the street.

I snapped off another shot, sending it along with

more hope than aim. The slug struck the pavement close to the mustached man's foot, then careened into space with an eerie whine. The man spread out on the street scrambled to his feet and disappeared behind a rolling cloud of black smoke.

The remaining member of the assassination team turned momentarily. His penetrating eyes shaded by eyebrows as thick as his black mustache, glared defiantly in my direction. He discharged the final rounds from his battered-stock weapon, firing from the hip. The short burst forced me back down against the floor. But not before I memorized the would-be killer's face.

The fleeting glimpse I got of him as he fled from the scene was enough to burn his appearance into my brain. His narrow, sallow-skinned face with sunken cheeks was split by a long, extremely thin nose. His hair was straight and dull black in color. The stub end of a slim, black cheroot was clamped tightly between his thin, grim lips. It was remarkable that he had kept it clenched between his teeth throughout his desperate movements. The dark suit, white shirt, and black string tie he wore completed an amazing resemblance to the traditional appearance of a turn-of-the-century mortician. From this point on, I'd think of him as an undertaker.

I got to my feet. The opposite side of the street looked like a stage setting for a Dante's *Inferno* scene. Within minutes fire equipment and police would arrive. Before then, the car would become a burned-out hulk. The luckless driver's body would be almost entirely consumed. The nauseous odor of broiling human flesh was unmistakable.

I looked over my shoulder toward Fumiere, steeling myself for what I expected to see. He was slumped forward. Even before I pushed back his head to stare into his vacant eyes, I knew that no man could lose so much blood as was soaking his chest and still be alive. The three holes in his huge chest were small, but the bullets that struck him were of the dum-dum variety. Most of Fumiere's backbone and lungs were matted to the mesh of his cane-back wheelchair. When I let his head fall forward again, his whole body followed, landing facedown on the blood-slippery floor.

The scanty information given to me by Fumiere was a thin lead. Someone—the undertaker—had made sure that I would learn nothing more from the now-lifeless cripple. The first solid link in a chain I hoped would lead to Randolph had been destroyed.

The wail of an approaching siren blended with the hoot of a police car to produce a synergetic symphony not far away. It took the insistent clang of a fire truck bell, though, to prod me off dead center. Across the street, billows of smoke and tongues of bright flame were vying for dominance in and around the two burning stores. A muffled explosion inside the wine shop was followed by another, more powerful blast.

I turned my back and hunched my shoulders.

The jagged remnants of glass clinging to the frame work of Fumiere's storefront window flew past me.

It was time to leave.

I went through the door in a partition blocking off the rear of the shop. It opened into a cluttered back room. The increased volume of a police car siren told me that the first cruiser had turned the near corner. The sound of the clanging fire bell also was growing closer rapidly.

I stuck my head out of the back door and looked up and down the alley. It was clear in both directions. I stepped outside and turned right. After five paces, I drew up short. A fire truck swung into the alley ahead of me and came to a halt. It blocked that end of the debris-littered passageway.

I retreated, slipping back into the rear of Fumiere's shop. In a few moments the entire area would be cordoned off. The sawhorse barriers would keep curious spectators at a safe distance. But it would also trap inside anyone attempting to leave the scene. Strangers would be especially suspect.

My American-style clothes were a sure giveaway. In addition, they were soiled and blood-flecked. For the first time I noticed a rivulet of my own blood running across the back of my left hand. One of the flying shards of glass had pierced my jacket sleeve and slashed my upper arm. I hadn't felt it at the time. There was no time to concern myself with it now.

Next to the rear exit door I found a dark beret and a loose-fitting trademan's smock. The impromptu disguise bolstered my confidence only slightly, but it was better than none. My proficiency in the French language should get me past all but a prolonged or detailed interrogation should I be stopped.

My nerves were much less tense after I had put three blocks behind me. The brisk walk had also given me time to reflect. So did the doorway I ducked into where I could peel off the smock and my jacket underneath. My shirt sleeve was blotted with a red smear. I rolled it up and bound my handerchief tightly around the minor wound. it was a toss-up whether the deep scratch needed a stitch or not.

What really bothered me was the question of the role Fumiere played in the game involving Randolph. The Frenchman's death could have been an accident. He could have been a victim of miscalculation, his own phone call bringing in the heavy guns and then finding himself unable to get out of the way soon enough. If he played the Judas goat, he would be expected to hold me in place as a target until his car-borne companions arrived to waste me.

Looking back, I remembered how close his own shotgun blast had come. Operating from a wheelchair introduces severe handicaps for a would-be hit man. But to miss from only six feet away?

Unless I'm absolutely positive, I tend to view situations in their most suspect interpretation. I've seen misplaced trust back-fire with disastrous results too many times. Still, I was inclined in this case to believe Fumiere had been truthful with me. The picture I was building in my mind would be much clearer, however, if only I had learned whom Fumiere had called on the telephone.

I left the shelter of the doorway and began walking again. I was on Rue Pardeaux in the St. Germain des Pres section where some of the most prominent *haute couture* houses are located.

A cold air mass had moved in from the Atlantic.

Thick clouds blanketed the city. The temperature dropped. Moisture came down in the form of a disagreeable mist. I drew the collar of my jacket up around my neck and kept going. Walking is good therapy for clearing up muddled thinking.

I had a lot to think about. If I had been lured into a trap, who had set it up? Randolph was the intended victim, really. I was merely a surrogate. Unless I was to be victim number two.

It wasn't too farfetched to imagine that Randolph himself was trying to pull a disappearing act and was taking desperate steps to cut off pursuit. But I couldn't conceive his hiring a gang of gunmen for that purpose. Unless he had gone over to the other side. In that case, it was easy to accept the use of professionals headed by a cool, funereal man who could kill while chomping a cigar butt.

The beret on my head was getting soggy. The light mist turned into a gentle but steady rain. I flagged down a cab cruising along Rue Claude Bernard. The ride to Rue Laverrier lasted five minutes. The dry warmth inside the taxi and the sizzle of its tires rolling over wet pavement were sleep-inducing. Jet lag was having a telling effect on me. I would have dozed except unanswered questions kept hammering away in my mind. For one, I had to decide whether I'd reached the end of my trail when Fumiere reached his. I also had to gamble on whether he had given me an honest lead in supplying a follow-up clue that would take me to the other side of the city.

I had plenty of time between now and nine o'clock to plan a course of action. The choices were few and simple. I could go to the Rue Hendrix address or I could forget the whole thing.

The Place de la Dujon district on the eastern edge of Montmartre was relatively unfamiliar to me. I knew it to be an old residential section where fine homes built in the 1850s once occupied large tracts of land. Since then, many buildings—mostly duplexes and three-story flats—had mushroomed on estates as the original, wealthy landowners sold their property to escape the influx of middle-class families.

A nagging thought surfaced repeatedly: Would Fumiere's last message lead to another ambush? It was difficult to concentrate while only half-awake. As the taxi turned into Rue Laverrier, I settled one point. I needed sleep to wipe away my fatigue. Once refreshed, I told myself, I would be able to make keen, logical decisions. In reality, I was procrastinating. I already knew what I would do. I couldn't disappoint Hawk. He'd never accept my giving up because someone—Randolph's new allies, or Randolph's enemies—was doing their best to turn me into a corpse.

When I paid off the taxi driver in front of No. 247, my back was toward the building. The cabbie paid no attention to the francs I placed in his hand. "Look there, monsieur," he said. "Behind you. What is going on?"

The street entrance door behind me was open wide. A cluster of people filled the tile-floored lobby.

I disregarded the cabman's rhetorical question and eased myself inside to stand at the fringe of the crowd. About fifteen onlookers were facing toward the elevator shaft. The passenger cab had been lowered so that its roof was almost level with the lobby floor.

The taxi driver shoved me sideways to get closer. I lurched toward a plump woman spectator. To keep from bumping into her, I extended my hands. They pressed lightly against her upper arm and back before I could draw away. My hip brushed against hers. "*Pardonnez moi*," I said in a quick whisper.

The woman had thrust out her own hand protectively when she sensed someone surging against her side. The flat of her hand came in contact with my upper thigh, encountering more muscle than she had anticipated. Her head snapped around. When she saw and was pleased by the looks of her accoster, her frown of shocked annoyance turned into a warm smile.

She was an attractive woman at that in-between age when youthful beauty mellows into middle-aged maturity. The abrupt change in her attitude was reflected by the sparkle of excitement that lit up her lively blue eyes. When I drew back from the accidental encounter, she leaned against me deliberately. Her action was as bold as the unmistakable invitation I could read in her expectant face. I avoided giving her any encouragement by focusing my attention on the elevator shaft.

"*Eet* is exciting, no?" the woman whispered to me in highly accented English.

She remained close, her ample breast nudging my arm. She was well-dressed; the richly embroidered kaftan she wore was an expensive item. So were the rings on the fingers of the hand that clung to my left biceps possessively. When I glanced down to make note of that fact, her coy smile widened into one of anticipatory eagerness. I couldn't pull away without being extremely rude.

"You *aire ze* new man on *ze* fifth floor, *n'est-ce pas?*" she announced proudly as if staking a claim. "I watch you arrive thees morning." She squeezed my arm coquettishly.

"I am only visiting a friend," I replied noncommittally.

"You see? You see!" she exclaimed. "*Eet* is a body *zay* take from *ze* elevator." She shuddered with a spasm that had nothing to do with fright or disgust. It was purely a sexual response.

This otherwide sophisticated-appearing woman apparently had a peculiar erotic hang-up that was brought to the surface by acts of violence. Her hand moved nervously up and down my arm, then began tugging it rhythmically against her breast. Her eyes burned with a strange inner fire. It was a strange way for her to get her kicks, but then there are all kinds of concupiscent women in this world. I've run across quite a few.

It was difficult to see over the heads of the bystanders in front of me, but there was no mistaking the two uniformed gendarmes working to free a twisted figure from the gears and cabling that hoisted and lowered the elevator cab. My latched-on companion was standing on tiptoe and breathing rapidly as if she was fighting off a sudden attack of asthma. I became conscious of her knee and thigh seesawing against the back of my leg. I was on the verge of disengaging myself with firmness when one of the bent-over policemen moved to one side.

My view was no longer blocked. I got a glimpse of the rag doll figure they were trying to free. The blood-soaked victim was Ralph Springer.

I tensed involuntarily. The aroused woman beside me thought I was responding to her blatant advances. She took my hand. "You come *wiz* me, no? I take you upstairs to my rooms. You will like what we can do together."

I backed away from the crowd to be free of her. She misunderstood again, following with willingness. I tried to turn the situation to my advantage. I chose a far corner to talk to her. "What do you know about all this?" I asked.

"You come upstairs and I give you answers and *anyzing* else you wish," she promised huskily.

"Tell me here," I said sharply. "What happened. I must know right now."

She saw that I was not going to move until I got an explanation. "*Ze* elevator . . . *eet* became, how you say, stuck! When *ze* concierge look to see what was wrong, *zat* man, *ze* dead one, his leg was caught in *ze* gears. *Een* death, you know, *ze* body can move. You understand?"

"Yes. Rigor mortis action," I clarified.

"*Ze* man, he fall, I guess. From way up. *Zere* was so much blood, though. You can see if you look where it drips on *ze* floor." She shuddered again, then pulled at my arm. "Come—we can go up *ze* stairs this way. I have wine and pleasant ways to spend a rainy afternoon."

I pried her hand loose. It took some strength. Her original dark frown reappeared. "I'm crazy to postpone such promising delights," I consoled her, "but there is something I must attend to first."

She locked onto my arm again, this time wrapping both hands solidly around it. Her hips ground against my thigh. "You come wiz me now," she insisted in a pleading tone.

"Later," I promised falsely. "What's your apartment number?"

"No! We go up together now!" Her voice bubbled up loudly.

The confrontation was reaching a crisis point. One thing I didn't need was to attract attention. That would surely lead to questions. I was the only American present. My alien nationality alone linked me with Springer. I had to make myself scarce. I broke away from the determined woman, whispering, "Wait for me, *ma chérie*. I'll be right back."

As I started for the street door, the woman let out an ear-splitting shriek.

"That man there!" she screamed. "He was fighting in the street this morning with the man who is now dead!"

A dozen hands seized me. I wasn't going anywhere.

The curse I muttered under my breath was directed at whoever had coined that adage about a woman scorned. He hadn't made the axiom strong enough. But then he probably had never run into a turned-on, French, self-styled femme fatale.

FIVE

"Is that true?" The short, portly man who looked up at me with a cherub's face was flanked by two uniformed policemen. His chubby features, topped by a black derby made him look so much like the famous comedian, Oliver Hardy, that I almost made the mistake of smiling. His short mustache, however, was not rectangular; it was waxed to pointy ends. They twitched as he pursed his mouth.

I interpreted the antennalike movement as a sign of impatience. I looked down pointedly at the gendarme's hand clamped to my arm.

"Release him," the stocky man wearing a rumpled business suit barked in French. My captor let me go. "Now, sir," the Oliver Hardy replica resumed in crisp English, "know that I am Inspector Phillippe Du Brau, Prefecture of Police." He drew a leather case from his coat pocket and exhibited an impressive-looking badge. "You are acquainted with the victim?"

"Could we step away from this crowd?" I asked in a respectful tone.

Du Brau's mustache ends quivered. He brushed a hand in the air to indicate I should move to the far wall. I stepped backward and almost bumped into a man coming down the stairs. "Yes, Gaston?" Du Brau acknowledged the man's arrival. The plainsclothesman stepped around me and whispered something to the inspector. Du Brau made some remark in return, then gestured for me to precede him up the stairs. His man, Gaston, remained behind to talk with the cabdriver.

The stairs were steep. Neither of us spoke on the way up; we saved our breath for the climb. Du Brau was puffing when we reached the fifth floor.

The door to Randolph's apartment had not been forced, but signs of a struggle were evident in both rooms. I couldn't see any blood, but Du Brau said aloud what I was thinking. "It appears that that poor soul did not die easily or very quickly." To myself I added: Springer certainly had talked, and probably screamed. Du Brau said over his shoulder, "Now, *mon ami*, what can you tell me about this unfortunate person?"

It was pointless to try to fabricate something so I gave a brief, honest account of my arrival at Orly Airport, being met by Springer, and being brought to the Rue Laverrier apartment. For a moment I toyed with the idea of claiming that I presumed the apartment belonged to Springer in order to draw Du Brau away from becoming curious about the missing Randolph. Instead, I avoided saying whose apartment it was. Inspector Du Brau's sharp eyes darted about the apartment as he listened. They flared momentarily when I mentioned Springer was a staff member at the U.S. Embassy. He seemed to accept my explanation that I planned to use the apartment, belonging to a business associate, while he was absent from Paris. If Du Brau checked, he would find that both Randolph and I were registered with the International Press Association and were legitimate employees of the Amalgamated Wire Services with full European accreditation. The only twist I gave to the actual truth was to omit other events of the morning that were somewhat out of the ordinary.

When I fell silent, Du Brau shifted his penetrating gaze to me. I tried to read what he was thinking by the look in his eyes. I found no message there. His cold, deep stare suggested that a maze of shiny brass wheels were spinning under the dome of his derby hat. "How do I address you?" he asked.

"Just Carter. Nick Carter."

"May I see your passport, Mr. Carter?"

My hand was inside my jacket before I remembered Springer had taken my passport from me to expedite my passage through French customs. He hadn't given it back. This could get embarrassing. I put on my most innocent face and described what had happened.

Du Brau turned away without comment when Gaston rapped on the door frame. He stood in the dimly lit hallway with the taxi driver, beret in hand, next to him. After a few words, Du Brau dismissed both. I didn't like the look Gaston flashed at me as he gave a negative nod of his head in answer to one of the inspector's questions.

Du Brau's voice had a slightly sharper edge when he faced me again. "I regret, Mr. Carter, that we will have to detain you until we can verify certain statements you have made about your friend."

"He wasn't my friend. I saw him for the first time when he met me at the airport."

"Nevertheless, there are prescribed procedures I must follow."

"Am I under arrest?"

"Of course not. This is just a matter of form. I must ask you to remain in my company, however, until I can consult with your embassy authorities, but not from here. I must first confirm the dead man's identity. It seems he was not carrying any passports—neither his own nor yours—so we only have your word at this point as to who he was." He didn't add that I also lacked proof of who I was. He didn't have to. I knew I was in trouble.

"The passports were taken by whoever killed him," I concluded.

"Possibly—even likely," Du Brau answered noncommittally, as if making conversation rather than agreeing with me.

From that moment on, Du Brau treated me with little warmth although he remained officially polite. When we left the apartment building, the lobby had been cleared of spectators. Springer's body lay on a folding canvas litter covered with a coarse gray blanket. A single gendarme stood waiting beside it. He straightened his sloppy posture as Inspector Du Brau passed by.

I was placed in the rear seat of the police car next to Gaston. Du Brau sat in front next to the driver.

During the ominously silent ride I mentally retraced my movements of the morning. I wondered if, in time, Du Brau could develop a connection between my actions and Springer's death. He already had one witness who had seen our confrontation in the street. That supported my blurted-out statement that we weren't exactly friends. I'd have to have a convincing argument when Du Brau got around to asking about that.

I was sure he wouldn't be able to relate the nasty business on Rue Tournefort where the Undertaker and his killers had snuffed Fumiere to their earlier surprise visit in Randolph's apartment where Springer's resistance threshold had been ruptured. He'd been subjected to painful stimuli before he had disclosed where I was headed. It would take some digging before Du Brau unearthed that connection. While I felt sorry for Springer, I also blamed him for short-circuiting the one lead I had to the elusive Randolph.

"You frown, Mr. Carter," Inspector Du Brau said, speaking to me over the back of the front seat.

I didn't know my concern showed. Among other things I worried that some over-zealous station cop would decide to frisk me and find a loaded pistol strapped to my side. That would really blow my tanks. I didn't rise to Du Brau's invitation. I covered my confusion with: "I'll be all right as soon as I can get out of these damp clothes."

Inside the precinct house I was seated on a hard wooden bench and left to cool my heels. Du Brau secluded himself in a glass-enclosed office behind a chest-high counter. Uniformed French police on the other side reminded me of Beau Geste legionnaires manning a parapet. The older ones ignored me. A pimply-faced recruit didn't. I caught him gaping at me when I lit up one of my gold-tipped filter cigarettes. The stubs of three of them were in the ashtray when Inspector Du Brau beckoned for me to join him in his office. The splotchy-faced novice pulled back the hinged barrier gate to let me through.

Du Brau was without his hat. He had a bald head fringed with black hair. The fringe on the left side was allowed to grow full length. It was combed across the bare crown of his head to provide a thin covering. The few strands were distributed over his pale pate. The air in the office was stale and laced with a sharp aroma of French cigarette smoke. I don't know what they put in their tobacco blends, but I can spot the piquant Turkish aroma easily. It was overpowering and cloying to me. "You're frowning again, Mr. Carter," the inspector accused.

I grinned weakly and nodded, holding back my words.

"No need any longer," Du Brau beamed. "The man Springer is who you say—a minor embassy employee sent with a car to meet you at the airport. He had called in to report that you and he were separating. The time of his call, linked to what we learned from the taxi driver as to where he picked you up, tentatively places you some distance from the scene of the tragedy. I'm curious about some other facets of this case, but since Mr. Springer was a U.S. citizen with diplomatic immunity, I've been advised not to detain you any longer. This is now a matter for our foreign office."

Du Brau was as smooth as lacquered metal. He was talking with his mouth, but the words coming out had nothing to do with what he was thinking or what his true intentions were. Despite his assurance, I'd give good odds that he wasn't finished with me.

I knew that for sure when he turned me loose.

He said I could return to the apartment anytime I wished. He even offered to have me driven there in a police car. I refused. I said I wanted to walk. I had gone no more than two blocks before I discovered the tail following me.

Nothing would be gained by going back to Randolph's apartment. Hawk would have to be advised that my little game was close to being derailed. He had to be told of a possible upheaval developing out of Springer getting himself killed. There was no way to gloss over the fact that I'd failed to abide by Hawk's stern admonition to keep things clean and quiet. I wouldn't blame him if he gave me orders to turn around and come home as soon as I could get Du Brau off my back.

What I had to tell Hawk needed to be done in private. The only way to insure the confidentiality Hawk would insist upon was through the use of secure channels of communications. I don't know what leverage he used, but Hawk had succeeded in getting cooperation from someone in the State Department who permitted selected N-type AXE personnel to use the secure embassy communications system in times of emergency. This was one of those times. The contact man in the embassy was Joe Corbin. I'd treated him to a high-priced lunch at Le Gatron on the Champs Elysee the last time I was in Paris.

My mind was so fixed on how best to inform Hawk of my plight that I was halfway across the embassy entry lobby before realizing I had bypassed the check-in desk next to the street door. My error was brought to my attention quickly when a broad-shouldered Marine sergeant blocked my path. "Can I help you, sir?" his deep voice challenged. His beard-blue chin stuck out bulldoggishly. He was spit-and-polish soldier-perfect. The marksmanship medals on his tan serge shirt pocket flap glittered in the light from the chandelier hanging overhead.

Joe Corbin's office was thirty feet ahead. It was the second door down the corridor and next to the stairway leading down into the reinforced concrete subbasement where the secure communications center and code room was located. "I've come to see Mr. Corbin."

The burly sergeant nodded toward the door behind me. "You'll have to check in at the visitor's registration desk back there." He placed a big hand suggestively on his holstered Colt .45 automatic. It has a snow white braided cord lanyard attached to a swivel on its butt.

I pitched my head outward to look around his muscle-filled sleeve bearing three stripes when I caught a glimpse of Joe Corbin partway down the corridor ahead of me. He had come up the stairs and was turning to go into his office. I sidestepped quickly so Corbin could see me when I called out his name.

The businesslike marine misunderstood my action. He reached out to detain me. His hand missed my arm, and his knuckles banged against the solid steel of my pistol strapped against my ribs.

All he had to do was to say something. Instead, he made the mistake of spinning me around roughly so my back would be in front of him. His move was so fast and unexpected that my mind didn't catch up with my reflexes until the six-foot marine was flying over my back. I'd levered him airborne with a reactive self-defense maneuver instinctively. He landed flat on his back. His breath went out of him with an explosive *Whoosh!* and he lay dazed and wheezing on the polished terrazzo floor.

I heard another gasp nearby, then a rising babble of startled voices followed by a sudden hush. I looked around me, conscious of being the focus of attention. Shocked and bewildered visitors in the embassy lobby viewed the scene with wide eyes.

Heavy, running footsteps coming up behind me broke the silence. I turned to see two Marines of the sergeant's guard detail launching themselves at me. I held out spread-fingered, open-palmed hands. "Hold it, fellows," I pleaded. "It's all a mistake."

My capitulating gesture and hasty apology were ignored. The leading marine wore corporal's stripes. I saw his chevrons clearly when I grabbed his reaching arm and spun around, flinging him away from me with an impromptu hammer throw. The moment I released him his charging companion blind-sided me with a body block that sent me reeling. It was my turn to have the breath driven from my lungs.

I couldn't keep my balance. I landed hard on one hip and a shoulder, then slid on the smooth mosaic floor, ending flat on my back and looking up at a wavering ceiling and sucking in air. When my eyeballs stopped jiggling, I could make out a pair of legs standing beside my ringing head. They were long and shapely, clad in sheer panty hose. I looked up their length until the sleek thighs disappeared in the shadows of a pleated skirt. My eyes then shifted to travel upward along gracefully flared hips, then through the valley between upthrust breasts to a beautiful face framed by neat, shoulder-length red hair. She carried a file folder in one hand.

The girl stared down at me, then at the scattered marines. She burst into laughter. I didn't blame her. The offhand acrobatics she'd witnessed must have reminded her of a quartet of clowns practicing pratfalls. She snickered at the sight of the two junior marines trying to assist the shaken up sergeant to his feet. "That Sergeant Harper!" she scoffed. "He got his pretty uniform all messed up." She glanced down. "You look ridiculous, too, down there. Here, let me give you a hand."

I grunted as I picked myself up. "I'm sorry I reacted as I did. Can you hold off these bulls until I can get Joe Corbin to square things away?"

"My pleasure," she answered, disengaging her hand from mine. "You know, it warms me inside to see someone put that pushy, ramrod of a sergeant flat on his butt. He gets a little overbearing at times just because he thinks he's got some authority around here."

"Can you handle him?"

"Don't worry." She gave me a searching glance. "You're friends with Joe Corbin? I don't think I've seen you around."

"I'm in and out. The name's Nick Carter."

"You're Carter? Then you're the one—" She broke off as her attention was diverted by the approach of Sergeant Harper. He strode toward me. His right hand held his heavy .45 issue pistol. Its muzzle was pointed at my navel.

The attractive redhead stepped in front of me boldly. The top of her head came up to my nose. A tantalizing scent drifted up to my nostrils. She set herself to confront the angry, clenched-jaw marine. "Better step aside, Miss Frame," the three-striper growled. "He's got a gun. I felt it. Shoulder holster." He spoke to the corporal out of the corner of his mouth. "Flank him on the left, Clem."

"Put that cannon away!" the girl snapped. "Don't you realize where we are! Or how you look? Right here in the lobby!"

The big man slowed, apparently undecided whethere to heed the plucky girl or stick to official guard regulations. His hesitation told me that Miss Frame was more than an ordinary file clerk. "I don't know—" he muttered. "I'm sure he's got a gun."

"Well, you just let me worry about that. This is Mr. Carter who arrived this morning from Washington. I'll be responsible for him."

As the sergeant reluctantly lowered the pistol and slid it back into the black holster at his waist, it dawned on me why—upon hearing my name a minute ago—the girl had reacted peculiarly. I waited until the marines retreated and the fire in her green eyes had died out before I addressed her. "You're Kathy," I ventured. "The Kathy that Ralph Springer spoke to on the telephone this morning."

"You overheard then. Yes, I'm the one. I'm also a fixture in the security office where I take most of the calls." She began walking away from me, then stopped. She looked back over her shoulder. "I'd better make sure you get to Joe Corbin's office," she smiled. "You're okay, aren't you?"

I nodded and joined her. I was thinking what she had said about taking incoming calls. If she received the one Inspector Du Brau made to verify that Ralph Springer was assigned to the embassy's security staff, she was covering the news of Springer's death very well. Either that, or her sensibilities were buried under a coating of granite. I had to know. "You know that Springer's dead," I said flatly.

I watched her mouth. There was a momentary tightening of her lips. "It's something we can't talk about. Not until the ambassador makes an official statement and the next of kin are notified." Her voice was a monotone. It carried no feeling. She sounded as though it made no difference to her whether Ralph Springer was dead or alive.

On the other hand, she could be covering up her sorrow. After all, she and Springer worked together. They could have been good friends—even lovers. That led me to think of Randolph. She would have known him, too.

Maybe she knew more about Randolph than anyone.

If Randolph was the womanizer Springer had said he was, he certainly would have done his best to get Kathy Frame into his bed.

I studied her pert profile again. She had smooth, flawless skin. Her lipstick was a glossy shade of coral that gave her full lips a wet, sensual look. I let her go ahead of me to permit someone coming down the corridor to get around us.

Don't ask me if it was a man or a woman.

I was looking down, totally absorbed in watching Kathy Frame's hip-rolling, blood-stirring walk.

SIX

Hawk's voice, beamed down from a communications satellite orbiting one hundred sixty miles above mid-Atlantic, came through as clear as Gabriel's trumpet. The barely audible background hiss was typical of scrambler transmissions. I chose my words carefully as I briefed him on the day's events. He remained silent until I got to the part about Fumiere. Then he muttered something unintelligible. When I went on, telling him about Springer and the intervention of Inspector Phillippe Du Brau, he became vocal. I was surprised that he kept his tone so even and controlled. He had to be miffed at me.

"I can't say I'm pleased, Nick," Hawk's stern voice admonished. "I distinctly remember telling you to use discretion."

I was glad I'd omitted mentioning the fracas with the Marine guards in the embassy lobby or that my passport was missing. Hawk's tolerance for mistakes is extremely limited. "You didn't tell me Randolph had been jabbing a stick into a hornet's nest, either," I countered. "I've run up against a no-nonsense pro with a couple of nasty slopeheads. It might point us in the right direction if you could get a line on him." I described the man.

Hawk listened with interest. "*Ummmm*," he mused, "reminds you of an undertaker. I'll see what the computer can kick out. It may take two or three hours. Can you stay out of trouble that long?"

I looked through the thick glass surrounding the soundproof communications booth. Kathy waited patiently, her face in repose. Her calm features suggested childlike innocence, but she was far from naive. She could hardly rate a position of buffer in the embassy security office without possessing intelligence and special training. When she saw me measuring her, Kathy smiled. Her whole face lighted up. "I'll keep as close as I can to Joe Corbin or one of the embassy people," I assured Hawk.

I broke off the trans-Atlantic connection with the uneasy feeling that Hawk was a lot less informed about this mission than he was willing to admit. The Undertaker had reacted to my being Randolph's stand-in far too quickly to suit me. I hoped that Hawk could find out who or what I was up against before ten o'clock. Until then I was free.

My thoughts didn't have to shift very far to concentrate on the attractive redhead waiting to escort me upstairs. "I really haven't thanked you properly," I said as I joined her. "Would you consider letting me take you to dinner?"

She gazed straight into my face as if looking for

the answer in my eyes. I got the strange feeling that conflicting personalities within her were debating the question. When the corners of her mouth lifted slightly, I thought I had won. "I'm sorry," she said at last. "I couldn't. Not tonight."

The implication that she might accept another time came out hesitantly. It was as if she really didn't want to refuse. "Then how about letting me buy you a cup of coffee now?" I suggested. "I'd like to talk to you about Ralph Springer and another man who worked here as a diplomatic courier up until a few weeks ago."

Alarm flared in her green, gold-flecked eyes. "Please," she said huskily. "I'm a little shaken up by what has happened. Perhaps another time. I've got to get back to work."

I backed off. It was just as well. A shower and a couple hours of sleep during which Hawk could dig up some pertinent data on the Undertaker would be time well spent. This whole business was so tangled and apt to become unraveled so fast that I'd be smart to grab sleep whenever I could.

After telling Joe Corbin where I could be reached, I left the embassy and hailed a cab. While the driver bulled his way through the disorganized Paris traffic, I munched on a flavorless, gooey chicken salad sandwich from a vending machine in the corridor across from Corbin's office. It had been a long time since the first-class Pan Am breakfast I'd eaten by dawn's early light.

Nothing made much sense. There was a definite security breakdown among the contacts Randolph had established in Paris. Fumiere's death proved that. An irksome question was how the grave-faced undertaker-type had got onto Springer and me so fast. If his Citroën had followed Springer's embassy sedan to Orly airport, that was one thing. If he somehow knew ahead of time that I was on my way to Paris, that was something else again. Then, who had Fumiere talked to on the telephone moments before he was killed? Had he jotted down the Rue Hendrix rendezvous address on his workbench note pad before he gave it to me? Would the police find it and wonder about it? Would the Undertaker have the nerve to enter the shop to make sure of Fumiere and look around? The raging fire across the street would cover such a move. If our roles were reversed, I certainly would have risked following up to give the dry cleaning shop the once-over.

Questions were popping up faster than answers when I paid off the taxi in front of Randolph's apartment building.

I glanced up and down the street before going inside. Everything looked normal. That didn't necessarily mean I had nothing to worry about. I glanced up at the gloomy sky. As I did, a movement at an upper window caught my eye.

The pungent smell of cooking cabbage or brussel sprouts filled the lobby. The elevator appeared operable, but I used the stairs. A light shone from the crack under Randolph's door. I stood close to it, listening. I detected no sounds from inside when I put my ear against the door panel. I tried the knob. The snap-lock latch was in place. It yielded easily under steady pressure from the edge of a plastic card.

The sitting room was dark and empty. The bedroom door was ajar. A band of light streamed through the gap. I tiptoed forward and plastered myself flat against the wall next to the hinged side of the door. I listened again and still heard nothing.

Wilhelmina came out of my holster as a prelude to my lunge into the bedroom where I ended up in a crouch next to the wardrobe.

"Oh!" A wide-eyed, scantily clad blonde sucked in her breath and sat down with a bounce on the bed. Her light-colored hair flounced around her gamine face.

She recovered quickly and pulled herself all the way onto the bed, drawing back against the headboard. A stunning pair of well-developed breasts jutted against the sheer fabric of her open-front negligee. She stared wordlessly at the muzzle of my pistol, then raised big blue eyes to my face.

Randolph's paramour was not what I expected. I rose up and walked to the bed, nestling Wilhelmina back under my jacket. "Hello there," I said. My throat was suddenly tight. I swallowed. "What are you doing here?" I spoke English.

"I ask the same of you," she countered, now smilingly sure of herself. "I am Collette Chambre." She said it proudly and gave no further explanation as though none was needed. Her voice was low, a mixture of precise English with marked French overtones.

Her smile broadened as she ran frankly appraising and approving eyes over me. The scenery facing me was worth staring at, too. Collette drew back her shoulders sharply, thrusting her breasts even farther forward. Her eyes dropped for a critical self-examination. "You like these? They mus' be handled gently."

I sat on the bed next to her and reached out. My

fingertips grasped a small key that hung between her smooth breasts on a gold chain. "All lovely things warrant special care and consideration," I agreed, toying with the key. "But some treasures should not be disturbed until it is known what obligation is associated with their enjoyment. I really would like to know why you are here?"

Collette's finely arched eyebrows bent into an amused frown that gave her pixie face a seductive look. Her provocative pout spread into a gleeful smile again. "I have come here often, and am mos' welcome. I am waiting for someone." She ran a pink tongue across her lower lip. "But I think, *monsieur,* that you are mos' welcome also." Her soft-fingered hand traced down my upper arm as she spoke.

I stood up. Collette's eyes brightened with expectation. She was a charmer, all right. But she was making things too easy. There were a few things I wanted to know before I got too cozy with this tantalizing vixen. "I'm using this apartment now, so I was wondering how you got in."

"Oh, *monsieur,*" she giggled. Her shining blue eyes examined me with merriment. "Would you not present me with a key if I promised to use it often?" She laughed softly again.

I couldn't keep my eyes away from her long, tapering legs showing plainly through her filmy negligee. Her firm breasts were still trying to fight their way free of the thin, restraining cloth. She was so right: Collette's fantastic body was an open sesame to any man's apartment. And so to bed. "All right," I concurred, dropping the question. I had others. "It's obvious you've been here before.

But why now? When did you get here?"

"I jus' arrive. No one see me come upstairs. I am here to wait for Jacques. I wish to show him the gift he gave to me."

I digested that. Jack, or Jacques to her, would be Randolph. "Ah—yes. Jack," I responded. "You were supposed to meet him here?"

"*Mais non*. No. He does not know I have return. I wish to make him a surprise, I say."

"I heard." I was having difficulty concentrating on the questions and answers. "If you have a key, why should your being here be a surprise to Jack?"

"I am jus' returned from being away," she explained slowly so I could follow her. "I hope he will not be angry. He told me to stay and he would come to get me, but I could not wait to show him." She lifted both hands and placed them so her fingers cupped her breasts lightly. "See! These are new for him. He gave me money and now...*Voilà!* The big ones! Aren't they beautiful? These are the surprise." She grew wary suddenly. "You do not know Jacques?"

Through the diaphanous garment Collette wore, faint black and blue discoloring was discernible beneath her ripe bosom. Skillful plastic surgery had bolstered her naturally-undersized breasts to a state of remarkable perfection.

"Jack is an old friend," I said firmly to sound convincing. "Why else would he let me use his apartment?"

"Of course," Collette agreed.

"I'm sorry to tell you this, Collete, but I don't expect Jack to be home tonight. He hasn't used these rooms for a week."

She seemed pleased rather than disappointed. "Then he is back at work," she beamed. "He was worried about his job when he sent me away."

"Why was he worried?"

"He did not tell me." She sighed and spread wide her arms. I gawked at the stimulating sight. "Jacques is not a big talker. We do not say much when we are together." She looked sideways at me. Her meaning was unmistakable.

"I'm sure that he did not waste his breath discussing business when you were around."

Collette patted the bed beside her with one hand. It was obvious that she preferred physical jousting to answering questions about an absent lover. No person I'd met so far could know Randolph as Collette had. I needed to maintain her rapport. It looked as though I was going to have to do it on her terms.

I sat down next to her and again lifted the key nestled in the valley between her breasts. Slowly, lightly, I used its tip to trace a circle around her right nipple. Her shoulders quivered. "Jack must have told you when he expected to see you again?"

"What kind of man are you?" she snapped. "I am here, yet you want only to talk of another man." She slid toward me so her hip made contact with mine.

"All right. . .all right," I said soothingly. "It's just that I hoped to get in touch with him as soon as possible." I gave her my most engaging smile. "Don't be angry with me, okay?"

She pouted, her lips pursed to form a moist rosebud. Her sparkling eyes fixed on me with a vampish, sidelong look filled with anticipation. Then she wrapped her arms around my neck and pulled me down, her whole body climbing over me. Her lips reached my mouth as her legs twisted around mine. She was strong. "We will wait for Jacques together," she breathed rapidly in my ear between kisses. "You will keep me company. Don't blame Collette, *mon cheri*. . .it's been so long. It is Jacques' fault he is not here when I need someone."

I hung onto her warm, vibrant body. I had to, to keep from being pushed off the bed. Collette pulled herself up so my face was cushioned between her firm, lilac-scented breasts. She moved both shoulders and hips restlessly, rubbing her whole length against me. Her erotic actions heightened my awareness and response which excited her even more. My face and ears were smothered under her kisses and a darting tongue. Her hands were busy moving and clutching. Her strength increased with her excitation.

I've been shedding my clothes for years, but I have never had such avid and fervent help as when Collette's teasing hands went to work. She even made removing my shoes a matter of erotic foreplay. She plied her deft, anxious hands and nibbling mouth expertly. I soon found myself naked beside her. She had somehow discarded her negligee in the process. I remained relatively passive, letting Collette arouse herself. Not all of me, however, stayed inert.

She sucked in breath audibly when I stopped fondling a breast with one hand and moved it to the inside of her thigh. My gentle caress on her soft skin caused Collette to make deep, throaty sounds much like the purring of a contented cat. The muscles of her stomach alternately tensed and quivered. I felt the warm space between her legs widen with a trembling, readying movement.

Collette's breathing became a rapid fluttering. Her strong hands pulled at me as she pushed herself under me. Her gyrating hips stilled momentarily, then thrust upward eagerly to meet me as I joined with her. She groaned softly and rhythmically as she counter-matched my movements. Held together by tightly encircled arms and locked lips, only our hips moved in smooth, heady cycles.

Collette surprised me. It took very little to heighten her delight. She was unable to curb her fast-building desire. She moved quickly from one rapture level to the next, hungry for a climax. Although she fought to prolong swelling thrills coursing through her, she was unable to ward off the onset of the final burst of passion. She was too keyed up and had been denied too long to hold back the fiery surge that erupted.

I knew it was coming when she stopped moving suddenly.

Her strong fingers dug into my buttocks, drawing me down hard into her and holding me fast. She took a deep breath, filling her lungs with short, sharp gasps. Then she stopped breathing. Her head went back, burying itself in the pillow. She remained that way, tense and motionless, transported beyond all world consciousness.

When the spasm came, she shuddered violently and cried out aloud. It was a piercing expression of ultimate release. For a full minute afterward her body shook and quaked uncontrollably. She clung to me, sobbing with happiness and serene fulfillment.

SEVEN

When the sexual earthquake subsided, I rolled to one side. Collette followed and lay on her side up against me, still breathing hard. "*Mon Dieu*," she sighed. "So good...so very good." One of her arms was draped over me, her fingertips stroking the hair on my chest.

I finally disengaged myself and began to get out of bed. Collette reached out to restrain me. "Bathroom," I explained half-truthfully. She let go reluctantly. I fished through my rumpled clothes on the floor to locate my cigarettes. Collette shook her head lazily when I offered one to her before I went into the bathroom. I took a lukewarm shower, then finished off with a cold spray to wake me to the realities of the situation.

Collette lay supine and languid when I came out to dress. She had pulled the sheet up around her. There was a faint smile on her smug face. The previous frisky sparkle in her eyes was greatly subdued when she opened them to look at me. "Please do not leave." Her tone indicated that she was deadly serious. "I do not want to be alone."

"Why not?" It couldn't be fear of Ralph Springer's ghost in the apartment. She had no way of knowing that anything unusual had taken place before she arrived.

"Because Jacques said it is not safe for me here. He feared for me. That is why he picked Switzerland for the operation."

"He made you go away?"

"*Mais oui*. I would not choose to leave him. Oh, he teased me about my flat chest, but when we make love I make him forget that. So it was strange when he suddenly tell me to go to hospital to be made big. I did not believe him at first. Especially to Switzerland when we have excellent facilities of that kind here in Paris. But Jacques insisted. And after I leave I think he wanted me gone because of his own trouble he did not want me to share."

"What sort of trouble?"

"Someone was—ah—pushing him in the middle. Not that—I don't remember the words."

"He was being squeezed," I interpreted.

"Yes," she beamed, remembering. "That is it. He was in what he called a tight spot."

"Did he say who? Did he mention any names?"

"No. He had no time to explain. I did not want to leave, but he would not let me stay. After I left, I come to know the operation was an excuse. I am only sorry he was not the first to see my new figure." Her delightful pout punctuated the statement. "But no mind, now. I do not miss Jacques as much as I thought I would. Collette is happy again." She reached for my shirttail.

I resisted her invitation to get back into the bed. "When did you last talk with Jack?"

"Two days ago when he said he hoped soon I could come back to Paris. He telephoned the hospital to see if I had received flowers and the little note envelope."

"Did he tell you where he would meet you when you returned?"

"No. I thought I should come here. He only say for me not to forget this." She picked up the gold chain and dangled the key on it for me to see. "It was in the note envelope with the flowers." Collette had a sparkle in her eyes again.

I reached for the key. Collete grabbed my hand in midair and pulled it to her breast. "*Ummmm*," she murmured, closing her eyes. "Come. Lay with me."

I backed off. Collette was ready again. She wiggled her hips and clutched my hand tighter to her breast. She was clever, all right—using the key as bait to get me close enough to snatch my hand. It took will to stick to my priorities. "I have to go out," I said in a low voice. "But only for a short while. I don't want you to worry. I promise no one will disturb you and I won't be gone very long."

She let me slide my hand out of hers. I opened my fist. The key lay flat in my palm. It wasn't the kind one would expect a girl like Collette to have. Not on a gold neck chain. It had a long, thin, tempered-steel shaft designed to fit a narrow-slotted keyway. A lock on a drawer file, perhaps. Or a padlock. The letters BG followed by the numerals 3715 were stamped on the handgrasp. I held it up by the notched end. "What is this for?"

Collette frowned, turning down the corners of her pretty mouth. *"Je ne sais pas."* Her shoulders shrugged. A devilish gleam flashed in her eyes. "It fits the lock on the Prime Minister's wife's chastity belt, perhaps," she giggled. "How should I know?"

Without taking my eyes from the key, I asked: "Did Jack ever mention a house located on Rue Hendrix? Or a cripple named Fumiere with a dry cleaning shop on Rue Tournefort?"

"No. No! I know none of these things. Why do you keep asking me questions? I tell you there is little talk with Jacques. When he make love, he is the quiet one. Even in the morning he would creep out and let me sleep. Only sometimes would I stand by the window and wave to him as he drove away."

The key on Collette's chain was not for an automobile ignition but it gave me an idea. An automobile can be traced. A trace can lead to its owner.

I had to do this right. Collette wasn't going to field many more questions. "Is Jack still driving that old blue Renault?"

"Renault? No. It is now an English automobile. A low sports car that he keeps in a garage."

My interest in the key entrusted to Collette was renewed. "A garage? Where?"

"Not far. Two blocks, that way." She gestured in a general direction. "It is a repair garage no longer in use. In the alley off Rue Lassevant. He rented it so his almos' new car would not have to stand in the street."

A shot in the dark, maybe, but something. Chances are that Randolph had used his car to go wherever he was now. But someone collected the garage rent from Randolph. Perhaps that same person could furnish a license plate number. At least that much, hopefully.

It was a start.

Randolph obviously had more than just cosmetic improvement in mind for Collette when he packed her off to Switzerland: She'd been sent away because he knew it would be dangerous for her to be around him. He must have been walking some kind of tightrope, but apparently that critical aspect was close to resolution. Otherwise he would not have called Collette and alerted her to be ready to return to Paris. That led me to think that Randolph himself was about to surface. The fact that eager Collette had jumped the gun could cause Randolph as much disappointment as it had caused me pleasure.

I had to admire Randolph's ingenuity, although shipping Collette to a hospital out of the country seemed a little extreme. A little expensive, too, I thought. It was, however, a reasonable and effective deception. From Collette's 'before' photograph, anyone could tell that she was a prime candidate for implant surgery.

Once Collette was gone, it seems Randolph had easily succeeded in disappearing and keeping a low profile. He had covered his tracks well. So well, in fact, that the man I called the Undertaker had mistaken Springer for the target he was after. Poor Springer. . .if he'd just taken my advice and gotten out of the way when I told him to, he'd still be alive. Because he didn't listen, Fumiere was dead, too.

It didn't take much figuring to conclude that the murderous man with a slim, black cigar jammed in his mouth wouldn't hesitate to put me in the morgue as well.

Collette was already snuggled down in the bed and half-asleep when I turned to look back from the bedroom doorway. "Don't talk to anyone on the phone or answer the door unless you recognize my voice or Jack's." I doubt that she even heard me.

Before starting down the stairs, I stood outside the apartment door in the dark and listened. I pressed the light button a moment later. Bare, low-wattage bulbs went on at each of the four landings beneath me. The electricity would power the lights for thirty seconds before the automatic timer shut off the circuit. I summoned the elevator. While it ascended to the fifth floor, I walked down the stairs. It was a precaution. Anyone confined in a four-passenger elevator cage moving at a snail's pace is too easy a target.

Dusk had fallen. The air remained humid. I knew that no black Citroën sedan would be lurking along the street, but I scanned each side of it carefully. Everything looked normal. Two men sitting on a nearby stoop appeared to be engaged in quiet conversation. One puffed on a pipe. Pipe smokers, as a class, are seldom violent, but I was wary, nevertheless. I kept glancing back guardedly over my shoulder as I walked toward the corner.

The alley off Rue Lassevant was dark except for one weak light on a pole just about where the garage was supposed to be. It was an old brick building sandwiched between two other neglected-looking structures that might have been warehouses. Both had boarded-up windows. The alley was quiet and had a look of abandonment. I was certain that no one had followed me, but there were far too many shadows and high, dilapidated fences to be casual about them.

I crossed the alley quickly to reach the garage. Its weatherbeaten, green paint-flecked doors were padlocked. The padlock was new. Despite heavy rust on the hasp screws, they were imbedded firmly in the thick, wooden garage doors. No entry that way.

I scooted sideways into the narrow gap between the garage and the adjacent building. A pair of shoulder-high windows in the side wall were coated with an accumulation of inner grime, obscuring my view of the garage interior. Neither window had a lock. None was needed; layer upon layer of paint sealed them shut. I used the point of Hugo to slice through the numerous coats of paint, freeing one window frame from its jamb. Still, it took muscle to force the window open. I wormed myself over the sill and dropped inside, then closed the window behind me.

The large garage had a stale petroleum smell about it. Very little illumination from the distant alley light penetrated the dirty window panes. I waited a moment until my eyes adjusted to the musty darkness. After orienting myself, I began moving over and around cardboard cartons, oil drums, and loose boards strewn about on the greasy concrete floor.

A faint reflection glistened on shiny paint ahead of me. I sharpened my focus. The outline of an automobile merged as I stepped forward. I drew a finger across the top of a fender and rubbed it lightly against my thumb. No dust. The car had not been stored here unused for very long. The sloping back of the Lancia GT was slick with a recent coating of wax.

After walking around to the driver's side, I opened the door. The interior light came on, showing keys in the ignition. I didn't like that. Randolph would never have been taken on by AXE if it was known that he had a tendency to be careless or forgetful.

I checked over the inside of the car. It was showroom clean. The owner's registration was missing from the glove compartment. It contained only a Michelin road map of southern Europe which included Spain, Italy and Switzerland. The other item was a flashlight which had weak batteries. They projected a feeble, yellowish beam.

Initially, I was tempted to flick on the car headlights to illuminate the gloomy garage, but decided against it. The flashlight, inadequate though it was, would have to suffice. I closed the door and was left with a pale, wide-angle beam. I swung it around the vacated garage. The double doors that opened out onto the alley were secured on the inside by a sturdy 2 x 6 fitted into metal brackets fastened to the side frames. Turning around, I saw that the building was divided into two rooms. A cinder block wall ahead of me had an opening large enough to accommodate a commercial truck.

I walked through the wide door into the second room. On the far side a grease rack was hoisted to full height. The fading beam of the flashlight grew dimmer, then went dark. I shook it. It was wasted motion. I was left in complete darkness. I stared into it, trying to confirm the impression that I had seen the figure of a man standing beside the raised grease rack. I was ready to hurl the useless flashlight or draw my gun if the glimpse I got actually turned out to be a man laying in wait for me.

When my eyes adapted sufficiently to the limited light, I could make out the vague shape. It was a man, but his fear-widened eyes could not see me.

He was stone dead.

It was Randolph, his outstretched arms lashed to the upper rails of the rack, his handsome face puffier than in the AXE file photograph. It was easy to see why the pain still showed in his contorted features. He was tied by the ankles to eye bolts imbedded in the concrete floor. The bastards had raised the hoist a centimeter at a time and literally pulled the life from the man.

The gruesome sight held me motionless. In the lapsed silence, several bold rats ventured forth. They had been at work on the body which I guessed had been hanging there for at least two days. A puddle of dried blood lay at Randolph's feet. It had coursed down his legs, flowing from his rectum. I hoped for Randolph's sake that the excruciating pain he had suffered ended with the snapping of his spinal cord and not from ruptured intestines.

A half-chewed, half-smoked cigar butt lay near the edge of the congealed blood. It was the remains of a slim-cylindered cheroot, and I knew who had left it there. It was identical to the cigar the Undertaker had clamped in his mouth when he smashed his way out of the wrecked sedan across the street from Fumiere's shop.

There was no doubt in my mind now how my arrival in Paris had been compromised. No one—not even someone bigger and tougher than Randolph—could hold out and resist talking...not with his guts being pulled apart.

I cut Randolph down and lifted his semi-rigid body up onto the tracks of the hoist. The rats would never be able to scale the grease-coated cylinder to satisfy their hunger. It wasn't much to do for Randolph, but there have been times when I did a lot less for those who had to be left by the wayside. An anonymous phone call to a distant hospital would give me plenty of time to clear out before an ambulance came to collect Randolph's remains.

I searched through Randolph's pockets. They had been picked clean—just like the car's glove compartment. The Undertaker was no novice. He had covered his tracks well. The discarded cigar butt would be meager evidence for police investigators, but it certainly pinpointed the culprit for me. The overworked Paris cops would probably attribute Randolph's bizarre murder to a crazed mugger or a weird cult of thrill-seekers.

I hurried back to the Lancia and jerked the keys out of the ignition. I lifted and laid aside the 2 x 6 that barred the garage doors from the inside. An empty oil drum that I rolled against the wall under the window made my exit much easier.

By standing to one side so the alley light would shine on the padlock, I tried the most likely looking key. It fit. The green-painted doors swung back with little effort on my part, although one did make a loud, grating noise when its bottom scraped on the uneven alley pavement.

All things considered, I didn't think Randolph would mind if I borrowed his car.

EIGHT

Anyone in my business would be a fool to walk into a trap baited with the time of day. I made my first pass along Rue Hendrix twelve minutes before nine o'clock. Four minutes later I drove past No. 93 going in the opposite direction. This time I went slower and looked harder.

The old house, standing well back from the street on a wide, terraced lot, looked like a setting for a gothic novel. Like others around it, the structure was much taller than it was wide. The architecture was typically late nineteenth century. The steep-pitched third-story roof was a sharp silhouette against thin, gray clouds screening a nearly full moon.

A light was burning in the foyer, masked and diffused by frosted glass panes in tall, twin-entry doors. Other porched and turreted mansions along the street also had lights on, mostly in lower floor rooms. It was dinner time for most families. From outward appearances the neighborhood was normal. I made one more sweep along the street, noting that it was narrow, barely wide enough for mini-cars to pass. It was also empty of all standing vehicles. That meant nothing. If I planned to waylay someone, I wouldn't park in front of the house he was expected to visit. I'd make sure I got there early enough, though...at least thirty minutes ahead of time.

Which was why I was going to show up an hour early.

I made one more circuit that covered the streets on either side of Rue Hendrix before parking the Lancia two blocks away across the street from a neighborhood cinema with a well-lit marquee.

The brisk walk back, ending with a turn into the service lane behind Rue Hendrix, got my blood moving and put me where I wanted to be. I had to scale a wooden fence to reach the rear of the house. Despite the cheery-looking welcome light in the foyer, I decided that approach was too vulnerable. For much the same reason, I bypassed the tempting ground-level windows set in the stone block foundation. Basements tend to be cluttered labyrinths with very unstandard floor plans.

Cement steps led up onto weatherbeaten porch flooring. There was a choice of two doors. One opened into an anteway off the kitchen. The other was an outside entrance to a glass-enclosed space that once might have been a gardening alcove. Stacked clay and ceramic pots were dispersed along warped wooden shelves.

Neither door yielded to my initial pressure. Both had inside slip bolts in place. Once more I put Hugo to use, prying away the crumbly, hardened putty around the window pane closest to the kitchen door knob. Once loosened, I lifted the glass out in one piece. I stuck my hand through the empty frame and fished around for the slide bolt. It was heavy, square wrought iron, and probably hand-forged by some blacksmith before the turn of the century.

The kitchen floor was covered with a smooth surface, either tile or linoleum. I was too busy feeling my way around counters, chairs, and work tables to bother about what was underfoot. The doorway to the serving hall and butler's pantry was a lighter rectangle in a dark well. I started toward it but stopped in mid-stride when a faint buzzing sounded ahead of me. A cold draft blew past my ears.

Before I could guess the nature of the sound, a grandfather clock in a front room began a deep, hollow chiming. Nine o'clock. The tolling reverberated down the hallway in solemn tones. After the second peal I moved forward, hoping the clock strikes would mask my steps toward the front of the house. With my third step a door slammed behind me. The draft blowing through the opening made by the removed window pane had blown a pantry door shut with a tremendous slam.

I froze until I heard excited voices pouring down the hallway. I ran ahead and burst out into the lighted entryway. Two people were there. One, a slim girl, was frantically dialing a wall telephone located to the right of the double glass doors. She had to stand on tiptoe. Beside her, facing me with an upraised cane, was a gray-bearded old man. His rheumy eyes blazed with determination. His age-bent back made him dwarfish in appearance, but there was no mistaking his intent to block any interference with the girl attempting to use the telephone.

There wasn't time to explain that I meant no harm. I had to interrupt the call, whatever its purpose. Considering my most recent set-to with Inspector Phillippe Du Brau, the least welcome visitors would be the police. The defiant graybeard was no match for me. I stepped around two scuffed-leather suitcases standing in my way to catch and hold onto the thin, bony arm as it swung down. His other partially-bent arm remained useless at his side. The way he stood with most of his weight on one foot told me he had suffered a stroke at one time. The cane flew from his weak fingers and clattered across the wood parquet flooring. I held off the fuming man with one hand while I snatched the telephone away from the girl with the other.

She clawed at me like a wounded leopard, her brown eyes wild with anger. For a moment the three of us engaged in a macabre dance, with the girl hammering blows on my upraised arm while demanding that I release the old man. Her screeching French was imperfect, but understandable. It was not her primary language. I couldn't get a word in over the loud babbling of the infuriated pair.

I finally had to push the old man aside so I could seize the flailing fists of the wiry girl. "Hold on!" I pleaded in French. "I was invited here. By *Monsieur* Fumiere."

My words went unheeded. I got a sharp kick in

the shins for an answer. Releasing the girl's wrists, I clamped both arms to her sides by getting my arms around her and pulling her hard against me. Some of the air went out of her lungs. That silenced her. "Now listen to me," I said firmly, my mouth pressed against her ear. "I'm not going to hurt you." Her quick breath panted against my neck. Her stiffness eased. "I was sent by *Monsieur* Fumiere, understand? Fumiere."

Her soft brown hair brushed against my cheek as she nodded. She had a healthy complexion, high cheekbones, and a childish, thin-lipped mouth. She now spoke to the elderly man in a Slavic dialect unfamiliar to me. He replied in the same tongue as he hobbled to his fallen cane and stooped gingerly to retrieve it. The tone of his voice remained cautious.

"You may release me, *Monsieur*," the warm-bodied girl said in her hesitant French. She was a teenager, no older than fourteen, if that, but emerging as an adult, mature woman. She knew it. When I took my arms from around her, she did not pull away immediately. She looked up into my face, her cheeks slightly flushed. Her lips parted in a flirtatious smile. "We did not expect someone like you," she said admiringly. She stepped back. The low-hanging, scoop neckline of her puff-sleeved, peasant blouse barely cut off an indecent view of her youthful bosom. "Just that a man would come," she added.

The old man came closer and stared up into my face. His left eyelid had a decided droop. "You are the American we are waiting for," he addressed me half-questioningly.

In a way I was. "Yes," I answered simply.

"What has kept you? You are late."

"Late? I'm an hour early. I was told ten o'clock."

"Too late," the old man insisted mournfully. He made it sound like the lead words of an elegy. It would be too much if he was going to tell me that Ulrich was dead, too. Then I wondered if he was testing me. He could be Volmer Ulrich himself.

I put on a bold front, using an arrogant tone. "The message I received from Fumiere this morning told me to be here at ten o'clock. I am to receive something you have for Randolph." I hoped that using the name would clinch my acceptance.

The girl stepped up to the old man and spoke rapidly into his ear. The whispered Slavic accents were either Hungarian or Serbo-Croatian. The old man's red-lidded eyes looked sideways at me. The gray head trembled as much as nodded, after which the girl spoke to me. "As Otto has told you, Mr. Randolph, you are too late. Professor Ulrich, my uncle Volmer, is not here." She pointed at the two waiting suitcases. "As you can see, we are prepared to leave." She made the announcement as though it would have meaning for me.

"When will your uncle return?"

Her mouth firmed into a closed, thin line. She glanced at Otto. "Tell him, Frieda," the old man urged. Then I saw that the girl was trying to hold back tears.

Otto spoke slowly, stumbling over his limited French. "You must excuse us. We are a close family. I am family too because I have served the good professor for eighteen years."

I wasn't interested in history. "It is important that I be given what I came for. Will the professor return by ten o'clock?"

Otto stared at Frieda. "You do not understand," he said, turning once more to me. "He is away now for two days. He is not coming home."

Frieda nodded. "At first we thought he was working. Uncle Volmer forgets time when he is with his test tubes and experiments, but even Anatole has not seen him."

"Who is Anatole?"

"A retired druggist who has a laboratory for analyzing medical tests, I think. Uncle Volmer spent much time there. He could not stand being cooped up here. I do not like it, either."

I glanced around at the high-ceilinged walls plastered with faded, stained wallpaper. Dark drapes hung over tall, narrow windows. The mismatched carpets were threadbare. They created dismal surroundings for an impressionable young girl. It had an abandoned, neglected appearance, suggesting it had been put back into use on very short notice. I wondered how many frightened and confused refugees had been shunted through what was obviously a once-active safe house. Dozens like it are situated throughout Europe, serving as temporary quarters and first-level interrogation centers for defectors being held incommunicado until clearance is obtained to move the human freight.

"Has he stayed away like this before?" I spoke slowly.

Frieda volunteered the answer. "Only once since we have been hidden here. He went to Geneva to the medical clinic. But it is not time for him to go again. Not for another month."

"He is that ill that he makes regular visits?"

"Yes. For some time...I think three years...he has been allowed a conditional permit from our country to travel to Switzerland for special treatment."

That cleared up the question I had about how someone from our side was able to make contact with Professor Ulrich in the first place. Now, however, as Frieda explained, trips to Switzerland were necessary only for health purposes. If Ulrich was obligated to give Randolph something, but for some reason had gone underground with it, the wayward scientist had to be located. "Why did you tell Fumiere to let me come if you knew Professor Ulrich wouldn't be here?"

"This particular time was set by Uncle Volmer some days ago. So we expected he would be back. And I must say, you took your time going to the dry cleaning shop!" Her tone was critical, but softened again when she said: "But I also understand you have to be careful."

"Is it possible that Professor Ulrich actually returned to Geneva?" I avoided mentioning the dire thought that had spawned my question.

"If he did, he went without packing a bag." Otto understood Frieda's answer and nodded his head gravely in agreement. Then the old manservant did a strange thing. He waved his cane at Frieda and snapped out some instructions in their native language. The girl hesitated but a second before she obeyed and began climbing the stairs. Otto used his cane again to indicate I was to go into the darkened living room off the foyer. This time I hesitated. The moment Otto summarily dismissed Frieda, the tiny hairs on the nape of my neck began to stir. It occurred to me that the extended conversation I had just had with Otto and Frieda could have been a carefully rehearsed dialogue designed to hold me in place. I had a sudden desire to clear out. Otto gestured impatiently with his stick. "Please," his scratchy voice implored.

I took a wary step into the big room. "I do not want Frieda to hear if your answer is no." His spittle-muffled words were difficult to hear. The quaver in his voice matched the constant tremor of the fingers of his useless arm. "Have you come to take us away?"

His question explained the two suitcases in the foyer. And possibly why ten o'clock was a limit set on the rendezvous time. I hated to disappoint the old man. "That is not my job," I replied. "But someone will do that very soon. I came so that Professor Ulrich could give me something. An envelope...a folder...perhaps a notebook." I made various shapes with my hands, hoping to stimulate his weakened thinking capacity.

"There is something, but none of those," Otto replied. "A gift from the professor instead. It is in the wine cellar."

"No papers? No documents?"

"I know nothing of that. Only that you should not go away empty-handed in case the professor would not be here."

That remark introduced an entirely new concept into my mental processes. "Is this bottle one the professor had with him when he crossed the border?"

"No. It is something he brought back one night

after working in Anatole's laboratory. It is stored in the cellar. Wait here. I will get the key from the butler's pantry."

I trailed Otto into the foyer and watched his bent-back wobble along the hallway. Movement to one side caught my eye. Frieda tripped halfway down the staircase and seated herself on one step, her feet placed on the next. She sat like a boy with knees apart and skirt hem hiked up. Her gangly legs and thighs were skinny. She wore bright yellow, ruffled cloth underpants. The display was not particularly stimulating; I had no difficulty ignoring it without showing complete disinterest. I needed all the friends I could get. "Will you stay here to wait for my uncle?" she asked.

That was a question I had been debating. According to Fumiere's arrangement, ten o'clock was the time set for the contact. Ulrich had another half hour to show up, but I didn't think he would. On the other hand, I was leery that someone else, less friendly, might. "I have something I must do elsewhere," I answered honestly. At ten o'clock I hoped to be outside keeping the house under surveillance. "But I will keep in touch by telephone."

"You waste your time. I do not think my uncle will be back."

"What makes you so sure?"

"I listen. I hear him talk with Otto. Uncle Volmer fears this place is known to others. He thinks the men set on his trail are coming close. So I think he runs, partly because he is afraid, and partly so Otto and I can be free to leave, which we hope to do tonight. Poor Uncle Volmer. It will do him no good. Those who pursue are more clever than a sick, old man who knows only about test tubes and dangerous experiments."

"How do you know these things?"

"I am no child," she boasted haughtily. "You Americans have not been able to keep secret that Volmer Ulrich has run to the West. My father thinks it clever that I run too, but now I think different. The Americans are just as bad. You care nothing about us. You just want what Uncle Volmer has in his brains."

"What would you have him do? Go back?"

"Why not? That is our homeland. He would not be harmed. His science is too valuable. He would be allowed to spend his final days in peace."

"And you?"

"I would tell them—"

Otto's rasping voice cut her off. "You are supposed to be upstairs! Away with you!" he shouted. "You have other packing to do!"

Frieda stamped one foot in silent protest before jumping lightly to her feet and flipping up the back of her skirt defiantly. I watched her spindly legs carry her up the stairs and disappear around the corner of the landing.

"Come. You must take your bottle and leave." He turned to lead the way.

We had to go back into the kitchen to reach the basement door. Otto used an old-fashioned bronze key in the lock. A rancid odor came up the stairs borne by a chill draft. A switch just inside the door turned on a stairway light, but the cellar remained dark. "Mind your head," Otto warned, jabbing his cane up against the low overhead.

A second switch at the bottom of the stairs

turned on three widely-separated lights. Their glow
barely drove back the shadows in the dank, gloomy
cellar. A scattering of sandy particles covered the
crumbling concrete floor. The soles of my shoes
grated as I crunched along in Otto's wake.

We passed a pair of unlit storage alcoves. They
gave off a smell of damp mortar. There must have
been a dozen more elsewhere. I pictured an entire
basement made up of creepy, dungeonlike cubicles
jammed with discards and trash, so I got something of a surprise when we went through a bricked
arch into a larger room. A half dozen wine racks
stretched ahead on either side, leaving a wide aisle
in the center of the room. A single bulb under a
cone-shaped metal reflector threw a pale disk of
light on the drab floor. The racks were lined up like
free-standing partitions, jutting out perpendicular
from either wall. Their tops came within a foot of
the low ceiling. A quick calculation produced the
estimate that up to two thousand bottles could be
stored in the vertical bins. There was space enough
between the parallel racks for both Otto and myself
to stand between the pair he selected.

Otto shuffled to one area of pigeon hole slots
where a dozen bottles lay horizontally with their
corked necks facing out. All were layered with
dust. Some were screened by a veil of cobwebs.
"It's up here," croaked Otto, pointing a gnarled
finger toward the shadowy ceiling. I stepped up
next to him. "Best you use the step stool," he advised.

I pulled the stool out from the wall and positioned it. I could reach the top of the rack and all
bottles in between with ease. The extra height

brought my eye level up to where I could read labels just by drawing a bottle partway out of its individual bin. I was fascinated. One was a light-bodied Bourgiel from Touraine, vintage 1953. Another was a rich 1947 Musigny and beside it a 1933 Medoc from Valeyrac. I pushed the rare vintage back into its place, then reached for the one Otto pointed out with his impatiently rapping cane tip.

As the old man indicated, it had recently been added to the cellar. The bottle was free of dust and cobwebs. In fact, the dark glass felt slightly oily. It had no label. "Hand it down," Otto ordered.

I complied. His dry-skinned fingers scraped over mine as he grasped the neck of the bottle. Both of us had hands on the bottle when I heard a scrunching sound coming from the direction of the basement stairs.

"Frieda?" I called out, peering into the shadows beyond the nearby circle of light.

For an answer I heard a loud shout, the pounding of hard footsteps running toward me and the sound of breaking glass as the basement window directly across the room was smashed in.

NINE

A shot rang out. It sounded as loud as a 120mm howitzer in the confined space. The zip of the passing slug came within an inch of my temple. I dove sideways off the stool, pulling Otto down with me.

The sharp noise I heard as we crashed to the ground sounded like another shot, but it was the wine bottle striking the concrete floor and exploding into glass splinters. Some of the contents spattered on my clothes. Otto and I ended in a heap against the rough stone foundation. The old man's skeletal body sprawled on top of me.

I pushed him aside roughly to free myself. His frail body flopped over and lay motionless. From the way his head lolled on his shoulder, it must have struck the wall hard enough to stun him. His breathing was rapid and shallow. There was no time to worry about his well-being now if I wanted to survive.

Wilhelmina appeared in my hand as if by magic. That was my first instinctive and instantaneous reaction. The second was releasing a shot at the nearby ceiling light. It grazed the metal reflector, tilting it to one side. In the flicker of an eye during which the light shone sideways before my second bullet took it out, I saw the evil face of Fumiere's killer and the man whose cruel torture had taken Randolph's life inch by inch.

I welcomed the sudden shadows which put me in darkness while leaving my assailants silhouetted by lights behind them. I saw two figures duck low behind the wine rack that stood like a wooden honeycomb between us. I sent a bullet through the wafflelike structure and heard a grunting gasp as both men fell flat. That gave me a moment to protect my flank.

I whirled ninety degrees to face the window from which the first close shot had come. A swarthy-featured head was rising behind a big-muzzled pistol being leveled at me. I snapped off two shots in quick succession. Neither was well-aimed. Their purpose was to force the gunman to retreat. Both slugs slammed into the stone foundation block next to the man's face. I saw him fall back, covering his eyes with his hands. Stone chips can be as lethal as flying grenade fragments. His heavy automatic dropped inside the window, banging against the concrete floor.

A prolonged, dull silence filled the cellar. I could hear Otto's breathing. I thought I saw a vague shape move beyond the facing wine rack. Next I heard departing steps. One foot dragged more than the other. I'd created a casualty—leg or thigh wound. That brought on a fleeting thought for Frieda's safety. I discarded it at once. I could do nothing, so I uncluttered my mind to concentrate on hearing and identifying sounds.

"Let us talk." The words came to me in calm, deep-throated English. They matched the gravefiller's appearance, being spoken in a slow, dirgelike cadence befitting a eulogy.

I wasn't about to answer. He was either a fool or had guts that were encased in ice. I could have shot at the sound of his voice—hardly missing at this distance—and blown his teeth through his brains. He didn't deserve to die that quickly. It was his arrogant boldness that gave me momentary pause.

"I have no quarrel with you, my friend," the voice from the shadows came again. "Are you listening, Mr. Carter?"

I hunched back farther against the wall next to the collapsed Otto. My free hand brushed against curved pieces of the broken wine bottle, my fingers coming in contact with thick, sticky liquid.

"There is no need for you to sacrifice yourself," the voice intoned. "We have come to collect Professor Ulrich. He is there with you, is he not?"

The reason for the stand-off became clear. The cold-blooded Undertaker had no honest concern for my welfare; he wanted Ulrich and he wanted him alive. I heard the distressed, anxious voice of the man I had wounded call from the stairway. The Undertaker acknowledged.

"Listen, my friend," the low-pitched voice addressed me. "Igor is now going to turn out these other lights. No one will move toward you. This is done so I may talk with you on equal terms. Do not attempt anything rash."

I closed my eyes, knowing he was not going to

wait for my consent. He gave Igor the order. I opened my eyes the instant I heard the light switch click. My adaption to the increased darkness was adequate, though not perfect. I focused my sight on the aisle end of the wine rack in an effort to detect any movement.

"Now, my friend, will you permit Professor Ulrich to speak."

"The man with me is Otto," I risked in a whisper.

"Otto Haldar? Let Otto verify his presence by speaking."

"He can't talk. He is unconscious and may be dying."

"And what of the professor?"

"He is not here. He has eluded both of us."

The silence returned and stretched out. I could almost hear the brass wheels spinning in the Undertaker's brain. An impasse had been reached. Except he didn't know—and wouldn't believe—that I had not met Ulrich, conducted our business and sent the professor away. I couldn't be left to carry away the information I had come for. The Undertaker couldn't leave without having done everything he could to better his chances for success in the future, even if his only trophy was an American scalp.

The impromptu truce began to deteriorate when I heard the Undertaker order his injured companion to return to his side. I used the foot-dragging steps to cover my own movement toward the open end of the wine rack barrier. I snaked noiselessly on my stomach toward the aisle, staying close to the wine rack's base. When almost to its free end,

I felt the structure nudge my hip. It was moving. In fact, it was tilting, and I realized that Igor had joined the Undertaker in trying to push the heavy rack over to pin me underneath.

I had to act fast. And if they hadn't had to let the wooden wall rock at least once to produce the momentum necessary to topple it over, I never would have had time to do anything.

I leaped to my feet, simultaneously throwing out my forearm to put Hugo into my hand. With its blade extended, I whipped my whole arm around the end of the wine rack in a blind, reaching sweep. I felt it sink into a yielding target. The recipient sucked in air sharply, then released a muffled grunt. It was the Undertaker; his tobacco-sour breath reached my nostrils. He reeled away. Another vague form, panting from pain and exertion remained braced against the swaying wine rack. I ducked back on my side and put all my weight and strength into giving the extra push that would topple the improvised deadfall away from me.

Igor was unable to prevent the inevitable without help. I heard his cry of alarm as he bolted for safety. The storage wall went over, falling into the one behind it. Dominolike, both went down with an ear-splitting crash. Choking cement dust clogged my throat and nose. The injured Igor screamed once more. I heard the frantic tearing of cloth as the trapped man freed himself, then the clatter of two sets of hurried footsteps exiting up the cellar stairs.

I resisted the urge to empty Wilhelmina's magazine into the darkness. I didn't want them driven off; I wanted them dead. It seemed, though, that I had lost my one and only chance. On balance, I considered myself damned lucky. I had been cornered. Only a wild, desperate thrust with Hugo had altered the outcome in my favor. The grim reaper I had nicknamed The Undertaker was a trained assassin who would never retreat as long as he was able to put up a fight. He must have received a deep gash that was bleeding freely. His back-up men had their own wounds to lick.

I crossed the cellar to where I could stand under the broken basement window. In less than a minute the sound of an automobile being started drifted up from the street. An engine rumble was followed by a mild tire squeal as the vehicle moved off rapidly.

Everything became deadly silent. I was afraid of what I might find upstairs. I flicked on my cigarette lighter to see Otto. His eyes were closed. He was still breathing, but the rise and fall of his puny chest was barely noticeable. I left him and moved as fast as I could to reach the stairs. I turned on the cellar light switch in passing and left the cellar door open so the stairway light would also shine in the kitchen.

"Frieda! Frieda?" I called, swiveling my head as I hurried from room to room.

She was gagged and tied to a dining room chair. Her blouse was torn and hanging down from one shoulder. A bluish welt under one eye was wet from tears on her cheeks. She nodded that she was all right in answer to my question while I worked to untie the dirty cloth used as a gag. I continued to speak softly and reassuringly as I undid the knots securing her hands behind her. I ignored her whimpering questions and turned over to her the job of freeing her ankles so she would have something to do. "I've got to look after Otto," I said simply. "The center light in the cellar needs a new bulb. Bring one down for me if you know where they are."

Otto died a few moments after I had pressed my fingers against the carotid artery in his scrawny neck to feel his pulse. There was a patch of blood on the back of his head and a swollen area at the base of his skull. It would take an autopsy to determine the exact cause of death, but I could be partly to blame.

The old man cradled the remnants of the broken bottle in his lap. Its thick contents coated his trousers. To my knowledge, there isn't a single wine made that has the consistency of thick maple syrup, nor one having the color of used motor oil. I had gotten some on my hands. The recollection came easily because now I felt a mild burning sensation where it clung to my fingertips. It was also drying on my flesh and growing increasingly warm as it did. The damn stuff was caustic and irritating to the skin.

I picked up a shard of glass that lay on the floor in a small puddle of the dark liquid. I brought it up to my nose. The odor was slightly offensive, giving off a smell reminiscent of hydrogen sulphide. It certainly wasn't wine. Now I knew why Otto had been purposely instructed that this particular bottle was to be given to the man sent to Rue Hendrix by Fumiere.

I grimaced as a chilling thought came to me.

When Hawk gave me what was supposed to be a

simple assignment of looking into the disappearance of a former State Department courier, he had glossed over what classified data Randolph was to transport. I remember Hawk saying something about it being vital to national security and Defense Department research. He also had remarked that it would have such an impact on weapons that a whole new concept in military tactics would evolve.

What he didn't tell me was, rather than blueprints or documents in an envelope, Randolph was to deliver a bottle containing a quantity of the end product. Some of it was eating away at the skin on my hands. The burning sensation at my fingertips was still there.

I turned and raced up the basement steps two at a time, brushing by a bewildered Frieda who stood at the bottom of the stairs, a light bulb in her hand. I ran to the kitchen sink, turned on the taps and held my hands under the gushing water.

I had been foolish not to have considered that Randolph might be charged with transporting an actual sample of Ulrich's discovery. With my hands cooling under running water I tried to reason why. All chemical compounds, regardless of complexity, can be reduced to a formula. In printed, symbolic form, the formula could have been transmitted by secure means, using a scrambled photoscan frequency. Instead, Randolph had been set up to hand carry a container of what most likely was a virulent, deadly substance.

Standing at the sink, I took in deep breaths and endeavored to sense any unusual physical symptoms developing. Perspiration dotted my face, but that could be a result of sudden apprehension. I told myself to curb my imagination; it was building fearful pictures of a terrifying weapon. Was Ulrich's brainchild a fast-acting biocide that caused rapid death when a droplet invaded the skin? When released in the form of an atomized spray, would it kill thousands in the twinkling of an eye? I could be the first accidental human casualty. No...that unfortunate fate belonged to Otto Haldar. The satanical liquid had soaked through his clothes penetrated the skin, and seeped into his blood stream. He had not lasted long once his lungs began to fail.

I drew back my hands and looked at them. The fingertips were fire red around the beads of water that remained on my oil-filmed skin. I was still on my feet, although I felt slightly nauseous. That could be psychological and entirely self-induced.

If it wasn't, I had little time to waste.

It didn't matter to me anymore whether Randolph's job was finished or not. Self-preservation took precedence over attention to duty. Or thinking of anyone but myself until I realized that Frieda was standing beside me, still holding the light bulb. She had followed my rush upstairs to watch my strange antics with wide inquisitive eyes. "Don't go down there," I said firmly. "Not now."

"Otto!" she gasped, turning away and heading for the cellar door.

I overtook her, but avoided touching her with my hands. I deflected her with a hip block and reached the door first. I slammed it shut and locked it, then put the key into my pocket. "We'll take care of that later," I said in tones that were clearly an order to be obeyed. "Go upstairs and wash your face." She nodded meekly while fighting back tears.

My first phone call was to Joe Corbin. He grasped the problem immediately. He deals with my kind of people often enough to know when an emergency exists. No questions were asked. No arguments developed. In a pinch, Corbin is a man of action. "It's almost five o'clock in Washington," he reminded me.

"He never leaves the office before six-thirty," I assured him.

During the five minutes he needed to alert and give instructions to the duty officer in the embassy communications center, I went upstairs and told Frieda to continue to get herself ready to clear out. It was even more important now that she did. Whether she realized it or not, her status had changed. She had lost Otto, and the Undertaker had found her. I didn't know how long I'd be in any condition to help her.

It would have been easy. The pubescent girl was already so frightened she couldn't think clearly. She was willing to accept any guidance. Only I wasn't thinking too clearly myself. I was at a loss for ideas. Any moment now, I might start hallucinating. My mind wasn't on what I was saying, but I didn't think she was listening too well anyway. Some pretty heavy things had been laid on her all at once. Maybe she'd be better off on her own, I thought, which immediately struck me as being something that ordinarily would never cross my mind. I had reached a state where my own well-being was paramount. "You just stay here until I can figure out what to do," was the inane advice I left with her.

I hurried down to the foyer and dialed the unlisted number Corbin had furnished.

"Two-nine-two, four-two-two-one," the answering male voice said.

"This is Nick Carter," I babbled rapidly, then fell silent. My own name sounded strange to me.

"Yes, I know," the voice replied. "This line has been opened to receive your call. The connection you requested is being made." The voice had a mechanical quality. The sentences were spoken as if by rote. "You will be patched through as soon as contact is locked in. Pertinent security directives require me to inform you that only clear text can be transmitted from my station to you. Your party in Washington will have been told as well before we make the direct connection. Please stand by."

Hawk's voice sounded less clear than before. It could be that my hearing was being affected. "What's wrong?"

"You know what Randolph was going to bring back? It's not in writing. I found the real thing...in a bottle."

"*Ummm*, yes," Hawk mused. "That's entirely possible. You've done well."

"Wait a minute! That's not the point. The question is: Is it harmful to plants or animals?"

All I heard was an electronic click and a deep space hiss. The link was broken. The next voice I heard was from the embassy. "Sorry, Mr. Carter, we're having difficulty holding the frequency. Sunspot activity. Hang on."

I hung on and watched the knuckles of my hand holding the telephone turn white. My tongue seemed swollen. My mouth felt cotton-dry.

TEN

An eternity went by for me before the crackling and humming in the telephone earpiece subsided. Then Hawk's voice boomed, "Are you there, Nick?"

"Yes. Did you hear my question?"

"I did. The answer is a qualified no. Got that? Negative."

My heart didn't slow down any with the news. "A qualified no?" I repeated. "You mean depending on conditions?" I wasn't out of the woods yet.

"Why does it matter? Wait a minute...is this an academic question, or—"

"You guessed it. I came in contact with what I suspect is the item we want. Are there any side effects?"

The connection held, but there was another long silence. I could almost feel Hawk thinking. "You've introduced a truly unexpected situation. We planned to build a working model from the plans to be delivered here. We had no idea you'd run across a mockup. Is the designer there with you?"

"No. He seems to be out of town at the moment. What about my problem?"

Hawk ignored it. "What condition is the sample in?"

"Sort of laying around in pieces. What about my problem?" I asked again.

"It's not in a container?"

"It was, but it got opened accidentally."

"It should be under an airtight seal. Can you salvage any of it?"

"I'm already sick," I said pointedly. "I don't want to go near the stuff."

"Just a moment." Hawk's voice was irritatingly calm. I agonized while I waited. When he came back on, he totally disregarded the warning that a portion of the circuit carrying our conversation was over an open line. "You inhaled some of it?" he asked.

"Yes."

"How much?"

"Only a whiff, but I don't feel very well."

Another wait while Hawk considered. The gaps in our exchange could only mean that he was conferring with someone on another telephone. He was relaying my information as I gave it and passing back answers as he received them. It boosted my confidence in Hawk to know that he was consulting an expert.

"You can relax, Nick, my boy. The fumes are toxic, but only prolonged exposure produces any serious effects. Get some fresh air. You're experiencing the kind of reaction one gets from sniffing model airplane glue, more or less."

It felt like more to me. I reached out and jerked open the front door to let in cool, night air. My head felt better after a half dozen quick, deep breaths. My ears cleared up—enough to hear a stair tread groan behind me. Frieda was easing herself down the stairway. She looked forlorn and lonely. I didn't have the heart to send her away.

Hawk had more to say. "We'd certainly like to have that item you've run across. I understand it will retain its basic structure indefinitely if kept under a vacuum one-half atmosphere or less." He hesitated. "It was, wasn't it?"

My fuzzy mind recalled the explosive POP! when Otto fell with the wine bottle. It was that same sound made by a light bulb when it breaks. "Yeah...vacuum packed," I confirmed.

"How long ago did the exposure take place?"

"No more than fifteen minutes, I'd guess."

Another wait. I used it to put more fresh air into my lungs. When Hawk spoke again, he sounded depressed. "Guess we'd better write it off, Nick. Too bad. You came close to being a real help. I thought you understood. The material is volatile and tends to deteriorate when exposed to normal atmospheric conditions, so we've lost it."

"But you asked if I could salvage some."

"That would be possible only if it could be recapped in an air-exhausted vessel before it decomposes completely."

"How much time do I have?"

Anyone else would have asked what I had in mind. It was typical of Hawk to accept the question as being pertinent. The delay was a short one.

"We're just guessing, but you might have up to half an hour."

This time Hawk waited for me. I turned to Frieda. "Do you know where Anatole lives?"

"Yes. Upstairs, above his shop."

"Do you know where it is?"

She nodded. "Otto sent me there two days ago to ask *Monsieur* Anatole if he knew where Uncle Volmer might be. It is not far. We can walk."

I turned back to the phone. "Sir, I'm going to break off now."

Hawk didn't let me finish. "I understand," he rapped. "Do what you can. I'll be here in the office. Call me."

His last words before hanging up were superfluous. Naturally, I would report back. I chalked the needless instruction up to a cracking in Hawk's steel veneer. He was stirred up about something.

I needed a metal spoon and a clean glass jar. Frieda knew where to get them from the kitchen. I removed the key from the kitchen side of the basement door and used it to lock the door behind me after I had let myself through to the cellar stairs. That would prevent Frieda from joining me if she thought I needed help. No good would come of her seeing Otto, either.

The spoon was unnecessary. About five ounces of Ulrich's sharp-smelling concoction was captured in the jagged-edged, still-corked neck of the bottle which was wedged upright between Otto's stiffening legs. I held my breath while I handled it carefully with my handkerchief-wrapped hand. The dark, syrupy fluid drooled into the glass jar. I screwed the cap on tightly.

I took one last look at Otto's still form before I left him. He had served his master well to the very last.

Frieda was waiting and ready. She had put on a frayed, thigh-length coat styled like a U.S. Navy pea jacket. The rough wool material was better suited for a horse blanket. Her suitcase was light. I shook my head when she stooped to pick up Otto's. "Someone else will get that," I said, holding the front door open. She hung back, uncertain. "There's nothing we can do here," I insisted. Frieda wiped her damp cheek and nose by drawing the cuff of her coat sleeve across her face, then stepped out of the house.

The night was still. A light drizzle was falling again. It was more mist than real precipitation. The street lights glowed yellow among the trees. Our rapid footsteps sounded hollow along the deserted streets. At one corner I looked to my left. The Lancia stood behind another parked car in the middle of the block, no longer reflecting lights from across the street. The theater marquee was dark.

"Just down here," Frieda indicated when I broke step momentarily. "That white painted building with the curtained windows upstairs. That is Anatole's flat, but he will not be there. He works through the night."

She moved closer to the inside of the sidewalk, then turned down a narrow lane running alongside the building. "The outside entrance to his shop is here. We must approach him carefully. He does not like visitors."

As I trailed Frieda, our path was brightened by the sweep of automobile headlights reflecting off the white surface of the building as a car turned the corner behind us. I lashed out with my hand, caught Frieda's coat sleeve and jerked her aside. It was a sudden, instinctive reaction that startled Frieda and made me feel foolish. If either of the passing car occupants had glanced down the passageway as they went by and perceived our jostling figures, they might interpret what they saw as a struggle between a mugger or rapist and his victim. I hoped our presence had not been noticed.

"It's all right," I calmed Frieda. "For a moment I thought that automobile might be turning in here."

Her adolescent face smiled innocent thanks. "Let me go first," she said and skipped across the cobblestoned alley. She was knocking on the side door when I got to her side. I heard the sound of a locking bolt being drawn back. The door opened to the width a safety chain permitted. A narrow, spectacled face peered out cautiously. "It's me, Frieda," she identified herself ungrammatically.

"Go away!" It was a demanding whisper from a thin, squeaky voice. "Your uncle is not here, I told you. I have not seen him." Weak eyes matched his weak voice. The corrective lenses he wore were at least a quarter-inch thick.

"I must come in," Frieda pleaded. "I have a friend who wishes to see you."

I stepped up behind Frieda, looking over her head so the band of light coming through the door gap would shine on my face. "Do you have a vacuum pump as part of your equipment?" I asked in much better French than Frieda used.

"What is this?" Anatole was curious. He did not

pull back or close the door because I held the universal "Open Sesame" before his eyes—a fistful of large denomination French francs. "I have need of your services. What you did for Professor Ulrich: exhaust a container in which the liquid will be placed." I held up the capped jar.

"I will undo the chain," Anatole said quickly, his eyes fixed on the money.

The door closed. It remained closed. Frieda tried the latch. The door swung back and we stepped inside. I carried both jar and suitcase.

Anatole stood behind a slate-topped table at the rear of the room. Twin barrels of a sawed-off shotgun pointing toward us rested on top of the table's flat, gray surface. Anatole's hand was around the stock, his finger on the trigger. "What's in the suitcase?" he wheezed suspiciously.

"My clothes," snapped Frieda.

"Put it down here in front of me," Anatole ordered.

I did, turning the suitcase around so the latches would be facing him. I also deposited the wad of francs within his easy reach. They disappeared into the pocket of his chemical-stained smock with a hand that moved faster than a cobra striking at a mongoose.

Anatole was very edgy and one glance around his laboratory told me why. To the uninitiated, the twelve by twenty foot windowless room could very well look like a testing lab. I knew differently. If Anatole performed clinical analyses on blood, urine and mucus samples for physicians, that part of his business was a front. What was really going on was made perfectly clear by the bubbling retorts, the complex distillation equipment and pill press on benches along the side wall. Anatole was up to his ear lobes in the production of street-quality drugs. It was a small operation, relying principally on tubular glass refraction units heated by Bunsen burners and other handcrafted glass devices. The clincher was the stainless steel mixing machine that once was standard equipment for drug pushers in Marseilles. Anatole was busily combining plain old borax or cheap lactose with refined cocaine and spitting it out in cellophane envelopes the size of ravioli squares that would weigh about fourteen grams.

After digging through the meager belongings in Frieda's battered luggage, Anatole shoved the still-opened suitcase toward her, then stretched a hand out to me. "All right, let's have your jar. I've got a stress-wall fifty cubic centimeter test tube that will handle the job. I'll run the pressure down to six hundred millibars like last time. It'll take about ten minutes."

Anatole carried the shotgun with him to the other side of the room and propped it close at hand next to the wooden bench where he commenced working. I shook my head and made an assuring face to calm Frieda's concern over Anatole's actions with the weapon. I didn't like it either. Anatole was much too jittery. He acted as though he expected trouble at any moment. He had a right to. Besides worrying about police busts, men in his dirty business had the constant threat of competition coming around to put his lights out.

Some of his nervousness contaminated me. I grew uncomfortable cooped up in the warm, chemical-cluttered room. "Do you mind if I smoke?" I asked.

Anatole flipped the switch which started the vacuum pump, then turned around. "Not in here, please."

It couldn't be that he considered smoking hazardous. A number of containers holding flammable chemicals lined his shelves. Demi-johns of alcohol and naptha were stored under his bench. "It bothers my throat." He released a nasal cough for emphasis. "Go into the front office. Through that door." His head bobbed. "Leave it open so you won't have to turn on any lights." The rhythmical thumping of the vacuum pump punctuated his words. It had started out fast and was slowing as the work got harder.

I lit up, the flare of my lighter letting me see my way around the office to the front door. It was solid wood, barred and padlocked. Windows on either side of it were covered by fully extended metal venetian blinds. I stuck my fingers through the flexible slats at eye level and pulled down, bending the lower slats out of the way to glance out into the street. It was empty. I released the blinds. They snapped back into place. At the same moment a shifting source of light moved partway across the blinds from outside then stopped. I peered through the narrow slit between two slats. A vehicle had rounded the corner and come to a halt alongside the curb. Its headlights went out, but no one got out.

The vehicle was an unmarked, solid-panelled van. It was a commercial model, and when a lights-dimmed sedan came coasting down the street from the opposite direction and stopped so that Anatole's building was between it and the van, I knew instantly what was happening.

A drug bust was coming down and it was my fault. I knew exactly how the unmarked van had come to be there.

It started when a stake-out across from the darkened theater observed a fast-walking couple out on the street at a late hour. One carried a suitcase that could contain laundered cash for a big drug buy. Then the furtive pair acted as guilty as hell by ducking out of sight when the surveillance team spotted them in the alley leading to the side door of a suspected drug supplier. It all added up to probable cause to call in the narcs.

It might take them five minutes to deploy and get organized for the raid. I hoped so. I ground out my cigarette hastily and put the still-warm butt in my pocket. I stopped in the doorway leading back into the lab. Anatole was at the workbench, his back to me. Frieda was beyond him, standing to one side between the slate-topped table and the rear cinderblock wall. I motioned for Frieda to stay where she was. She frowned questioningly. I double-timed by gesture. She finally nodded her agreement.

"Isn't that about ready," I called out as I walked toward Anatole.

He turned and bent down to examine the vacuum gauge. "Six hundred and forty," he read off. "Another minute," he predicted.

We didn't have another minute. A sharp pounding rapped on the side door. A voice beyond it, magnified by a bullhorn, identified the speaker as a police officer and demanded entry.

The weak-eyed Anatole reacted instantly. It was as if he had an emergency plan that he practiced everyday. He leaped for the wall and pulled down the fuse box master switch, cutting off the electric lights. The only illumination came from the blue flames of the Bunsen burners on the wooden workbench. In that eerie light, I saw Anatole snatch up his shotgun. I had made my way along the side wall and reached Frieda just as the side door burst open.

The first daring cop, wearing clothing similar to the dark fatigues of the LAPD SWAT team, popped up in the doorway like a jack-in-the-box. He spied Anatole holding the shotgun at the ready. A short burst spewed from the cop's carbine. Anatole staggered in his tracks. He hung onto his shotgun as the went down on one knee.

I pushed the slate-topped lab table over and ducked behind it, pulling Frieda down beside me. One barrel of Anatole's shotgun went off, pointing in the general direction of the battered door. It drove the intruders back. Heavy police fire rippled from outside. Bullets sprayed the inside of the lab. Slugs bounced off the slate shield I had thrown up. Glass on the other side of the room shattered and flew about. A second deafening shotgun blast went off, smashing into the side wall.

A *WHUMPF!*, followed by a glare of orange light, brightened the room. I risked a glance around the edge of a vertical-standing table top. Anatole's wild shot had struck and severed the main gas line. Three-foot long flames spewed out of the twisted end of a broken pipe. Anatole was down on his hands and knees, crawling aimlessly.

The lab was turning into an inferno. The French narcs were being held back by the flames. I heard hoarse voices outside calling a retreat.

The fire spread quickly. It now enveloped the workbench and covered the entire front wall, cutting us off from the front office. The guarded side door was the only way out. Much as I hated walking into the arms of the French police once again, my main concern was stepping out with Frieda into a hail of lead. We had no choice. We could not stay where we were; we'd be cooked alive.

I huddled with Frieda and explained what we might have to do. I held onto her small, trembling hand while I stood up and began shouting as loudly as I could: "Hold your fire! We give up! We have no weapons! We're coming out!"

There was no point in wasting breath trying to tell them we were blameless bystanders. We'd settle that later. All I wanted was for someone to hear that we surrendered and wanted out alive. All I hoped to hear in return was word that we wouldn't be killed as we stumbled out of the doomed building.

No one answered my shouts. They may not have been heard. The hissing and crackling of flames inside the burning room were hellishly loud. We couldn't wait any longer. No matter what fate awaited us beyond the flame-ringed door, it was now or never.

I hunkered down next to Frieda. "Are you ready?" I asked encouragingly.

She gave me a wan smile and nodded.

"Don't let go of my hand. We'll make it fine."

She nodded again, but her smile was gone.

I tightened my grip on her hand. As I did, the whole world around us became unhinged. The building heaved and thundered, shaken by a tremendous force. Only the sudden, chain reaction detonation of Anatole's overheated store of highly explosive chemicals could have produced such an effect.

The earthshaking blast shoved the underside of the heavy lab table against us as if it were driven by a giant hand. We tumbled sideways by its force. If it weren't for the table's sturdy legs ramming into the wall behind us, preventing the stone table top from slamming us into the cinderblock wall, we would have been crushed to death. The wall itself buckled outward under the tremendous pressure.

My ears rang and went numb. The ceiling bulged upward above us, then reversed direction and came down with a nerve-shattering crash. In the flickering firelight, diffused in a fog of plaster dust, my unsteady eyes saw that a whole section of the back wall had disappeared. Cinderblocks had been scattered like dominoes, leaving a gaping, smoking hole.

I still had hold of Frieda's hand.

I dragged her to her wobbly feet and led her outside to fresh air.

We had nothing but the singed clothes on our backs, but we were alive . . . and free.

ELEVEN

Billowing smoke made us cough as Frieda and I ran hand in hand from the collapsing building. A wall of roaring flames blocked the alley behind us. From the noises in the street, momentary confusion immobilized the police driven back by the miniature holocaust.

We circled the block at a panic-controlled walk and approached the Lancia from the rear. A canopy of orange fog covered the spot where Anatole's laboratory still burned fiercely.

We got into the car. Frieda huddled in the seat next to me, whimpering from mild shock. I cranked up the car and turned on the headlights. They illuminated a fatigue-uniformed figure posted at the street intersection. He hoisted his weapon to the port arms position and began walking toward us purposefully. Every nerve end curled up tight within me while I sat and waited.

The smoke-smudged face of the special officer peered at me through the car window I had lowered halfway. He glanced across at Frieda. I was figuring how I could bluff my way out of an apparently compromising situation involving an older man with a terrified, underage girl. The blackened-faced gendarme only smiled. "So sorry, *monsieur*. As you see, there is a fire. The intersection ahead must be kept clear for arriving fire equipment. You will have to go the other way. You understand."

"I understand," I replied, smiling back. I mustn't seem too anxious. "Did the family get out of the house?"

"It is a shop, not a house," he answered, backing away.

I nodded and closed the window all the way. The cop stepped up onto the curb. I made a reasonably slow U-turn, but speeded up as I approached the corner. It would be wise to get around it before the temporary traffic director thought to make a note of the rear license plate.

The marine on night duty behind the desk in the embassy lobby was the one Sergeant Harper had called Clem. From the way he looked at me sourly, I wondered if he was pulling extra duty as punishment given for unruly behavior. The rumpled, ragamuffin appearance of Frieda softened his stern countenance.

"I'd like to see someone about making arrangements for this young lady to be looked after," I informed him.

Clem knew his standard procedures manual well. He picked up the telephone and dialed an internal number. He merely repeated my request, then handed the instrument to me. "It's Mr. Slocum, the Third Secretary. He's the one here tonight to handle these after-hours problems."

Mr. Slocum was reservedly polite. He turned even more aloof when I mentioned my name. He'd heard of me. No doubt the afternoon incident that pitted Sergeant Harper against me had gone through the embassy grapevine like a case of Montezuma's revenge. "I don't believe you understand our position, Mr. Carter. We can't provide care and shelter to every street urchin brought in by some American citizen. There are established social service agencies you can go to."

I got a little huffy. "I don't think *you* understand, Mr. Slocum. Unless I'm mistaken, the embassy is indirectly if not totally responsible. I found her in a safe house on Rue Hendrix. Someone in this building put her there: Rue Hendrix . . . in Montmartre," I emphasized.

Slocum digested that for a moment before answering. Then all he said was "Oh." It came out a combination of surprise and relief. At least he knew what sort of machinery he was dealing with now.

"Well, Mr. Slocum?"

"Ah . . . yes." He took his time. "That's a little different matter," he admitted. "It's also a bit out of my purview. Let's see . . . no one mans that office at night, but one of them is on standby. The call-in roster is right here. Yes, her number is 292-4345."

"Her?" I pulled the receiver away from my face and looked at it. "I'm not talking about the Red

Cross or Traveler's Aid."

"I assure you, Mr. Carter, I know who operates the Rue Hendrix property. And Miss Frame is . . . ah . . . most capable in these matters."

"Kathy Frame?" I blurted out.

Slocum took a moment to respond. "That's right. You *do* know her. Well . . . you can be sure she is sufficiently knowledgeable to handle this situation. If you and your . . . your charge will be patient, I'll call Miss Frame and get her down here." He sounded anxious to be rid of me and a subject he considered distasteful. Career diplomats tend to shy away from self-involvement in anything that smacks of covert operations.

"No need for you to bother," I suggested. "I'll call her." I fished some coins out of my pocket and offered them to Frieda. "There's a vending machine down the hall. Get yourself some hot chocolate."

Clem interpreted my gesture and probably had picked up enough bedroom French while in Paris to understand what I had said. He jumped up and stepped around the desk. "I'm sorry, sir. That part of the building is off limits to . . . ah . . . no one goes down there unescorted after normal business hours."

"No one?" I growled.

"Well . . . ah . . . it's all right for you, I guess. But the kid will have to stay here."

I was getting no help from anyone and not liking it at all. Part of my problem was that I was dirty, sore and bone-weary. I still felt a little nauseous from inhaling chemical smoke and the fumes from Ulrich's strange mixture which I was beginning to suspect had nothing to do with improving United States military capability. My nerves were on-edge and I had to curb myself to address Clem civilly. "I suppose it's all right if she sits on the bench over there?" I said curtly and regretted it immediately.

Clem nodded. His eyes followed us as I led Frieda to one side. She was ready to break out into tears again. She had enough reason to. "Be right back," I promised.

While the vending machine dispensed hot chocolate for Frieda and black coffee for me, I told myself I wasn't procrastinating. Hawk was waiting for me to get back to him, but I first wanted to be sure that Frieda was placed in good hands as soon as possible. That I hadn't yet decided how Hawk should be told I'd lost Ulrich's precious sample had nothing to do with it.

Frieda thanked me for the steaming drink. I glanced at my watch. It was hard to believe it was not yet midnight. Still, it was quite late to be calling up respectable people and rooting them out of bed.

I reached for the phone on Clem's lobby desk. "You'll have to use the public phone over there," he said. His thumb jerked hitchhiking fashion to indicate where. "This one has to be kept free for incoming calls."

He was right, but I deliberately kept my hand on the telephone and glared at him challengingly. Clem started to get to his feet. I surrendered the phone before a more serious confrontation developed. Once more, I realized how frazzled and strung out my nerves were.

Kathy's phone rang four times before someone answered. *"Allo?"* a growly, masculine-sounding voice, came over the line.

I was a little disappointed. "I'd like to speak with Miss Frame, please." I gave my voice an official tone.

I heard sounds like bedsprings squeaking and the husky, sleepy voice, diminished by distance, speaking in English. "Hey, Kathy. Wake up. It's for you."

"Huh? Who is it?" her soft, sleepy voice asked.

"Some guy." The tone said my late call wasn't appreciated.

The phone clattered again as it was picked up. Kathy cleared her throat and said: "Yes? What is it?"

She woke up quickly and her voice brightened when I told her who I was. She grasped the predicament readily and talked openly about it even though her companion could overhear our conversation.

Kathy verified what I wanted to know in a few short sentences. "Yes. I know a little about that situation. Two older men. One has a daughter, but I didn't know she was with them. They were transferred to the Rue Hendrix house about ten days ago. It's time they were relocated. I think they were going to be moved on—let's see—today as a matter of fact."

"The men are gone," I said without going into needless explanation. The details would be known soon enough and had nothing to do with Frieda's situation. "I have the girl who got left behind. Someone has to look after her."

"I'll be right down." Kathy was wide awake now and eager to help.

"I won't be able to wait, do you mind?" I hoped I didn't sound completely disinterested. I wanted to talk more with Kathy. If she knew Randolph and had even slight knowledge of the Ulrich affair, her information could be valuable. I needed all the help I could get. I'd get most of it from Hawk, of course, and he was waiting to hear from me. He came first.

"You can do me a favor," I mentioned.

"Besides taking that loose female off your hands?"

"She's only thirteen years old," I made clear to her.

"I understood she was a grown woman. Well," she laughed it off, "I'm only on the fringes of this. What's the other favor?"

"Authorize me access into the comm center. My boss is waiting for me to make contact with him."

"Again? How much trouble can you get into in one day?" She sounded serious and sincere. "Put Corporal Tyson on."

"Clem?"

"Yes, Clem," she laughed. "I use official titles and military rank around the office so much that it's become second nature to me."

I wondered if she kept it up after she took them home with her. "Can't," I replied. "He wouldn't let me use his desk phone. I'm in the public booth by the door."

"I'll call him. And Mr. Slocum, too. Right away."

"I'm sorry that I ha—"

"All part of the job," she interrupted. "I don't mind. I don't often get a chance to get involved.

It's only because I'm the on-call standby tonight. Don't worry. I can handle it."

Clem's desk phone rang ten seconds later. He picked it up, then kept glancing sideways at me standing next to the desk while he listened. "Yes, ma'am. I'll do that. Yes, ma'am. Goodby." He replaced the receiver and lifted it again immediately. "You know the way to the comm center," he said while dialing. "I'm calling down now. Someone will be waiting to admit you." Clem didn't sound pleased to be doing something for me.

I recognized the code clerk on duty from hearing his voice during our previous conversation. He was much older than he sounded over the telephone. This time he introduced himself. "I'm Jim Atwell. Sorry about that interruption on the Washington relay before. We've been having circuit breakdowns all week. What can I do for you this time?"

"A reconnect. Same terminal as before. Full scrambler."

"Always have a Washington link ready," he said proudly. "Only delay is getting hooked up with your party through the secure switchboard in the Pentagon. No sweat at this hour, though."

With privacy guaranteed by the voice-coding scrambler, Hawk talked openly and freely. He was soft-spoken and sufficiently pleasant for me to brace myself. Whenever he hides his gruffness behind genteel speech, he's deliberately trying to take the bite out of what he is about to tell me.

"Well, Nick, were you able to save the sample?"

"No, chief, it didn't work out. There just wasn't enough time." That was as simple and as honest as I could put it without inviting questions and getting involved in extended, complicated explanations. "Have you got any information that will help straighten out this puzzle. I'm a little confused."

"I should think you would be," Hawk sympathized. "I'm partly to blame. I put you into this thing cold—and backwards. I want you to know that we didn't lay it on at all. A shadow group out in Langley wrote the scenario. We got dragged in at the very end. Up to that point everything was going smoothly and I had no reservations about cooperating on the simple job of taking Professor Ulrich's notes into protective custody and getting them back here. Langley didn't tell me that their spook network in Paris had been penetrated. That's when it went off the track.

"I've learned that Ernst Rutzmann was involved from the West German side. He was to be Randolph's contact. If a top man like Rutzmann was neutralized, it's reasonable to assume Randolph's out of the picture, too."

"He is," I interrupted flatly. "I've confirmed that."

Hawk reacted with a five-second silence. "Does that mean that you've reached a dead end, too?"

"I'm not sure," I replied honestly. "If losing the sample is the end of the line, we're out of business."

"Well, take heart then. That was a back-up factor. Professor Ulrich was providing proof that his discovery was worth what he's being paid. Just enough for test purposes to confirm that REAM is as effective as he claims it to be."

"REAM?"

"Short for Radiant Energy Absorption Material. That's what the Defense Department brass has tagged it. They're convinced it does it, too."

"Does what?"

"Absorbs energy. It's a remarkable scientific breakthrough if it really works."

"I thought we were more interested in producing energy than sucking it up."

"Yes, but consider this: REAM applied to any surface retains high-frequency energy directed at it, making that surface non-reflective. Understand? REAM absorbs electronic emissions . . . radar . . . sonar . . . infrared. Theoretically, a coating on an aircraft, submarine, space vehicle, any missile, or tank makes them immune to detection. Think of it!"

I already was. The impact was mind-boggling. Here was a counterweapon which would truly cause a revolutionary change in the world's arsenal of military hardware. It would make obsolete both offensive and defense weapon systems that depended on probing electronic impulses to seek out distant targets. The object, struck by the scanning electronic beam, normally returns a weak echo. That, in turn, is greatly amplified so it registers as a spot of light on a visual plotting screen on the ground which displays position and range to the discovered target.

Ulrich's REAM supposedly changed all that. His miraculous material somehow gathered in and disannuled the minute power impulses. No electronic echo was produced. The detection apparatus associated with the ground transmitter received no return signal. It was as if the searching beam had continued uninterrupted out into endless space. Perhaps it did. Maybe Ulrich's discovery shunted the arriving energy pulses around the object being challenged. To the equipment operator, no object existed—it was concealed by a cloak of invisibility. However it was done, the impact on modern warfare and weapons would be incredible.

Hawk had allowed me time to reflect upon and appreciate the immensity of his revelation. "I wish I had known all this before you took off, but it's been kept so hush-hush that I had to get a special clearance from the president to be let in on the project. Now we both understand how vital it is that we—the United States—end up with Ulrich's formula."

"That's not going to be easy," I predicted. "I've run into the competition again and they're tough."

"That's the other thing I got a line on," answered Hawk. "The man you're up against is Alex Brolaika, nationality uncertain. Makes no difference; he's a free-lance operator now. He's an old hand in the business, but crawled into the woodwork a few years ago. He's Soviet trained and every country in Europe, including France and West Germany, used him at one time. One by one they dropped him. He's not subtle enough. His methods are too crude and he's too quick to use unnecessary and unwarranted force. The way Ernst Rutzmann died is typical of Brolaika's methods."

"He left his trademark on Randolph, too," I added.

"The fact that Brolaika has resurrected himself points up the importance of Ulrich's discovery. A half dozen countries know in general terms what

Ulrich was working on. When he was coaxed into dealing with our side and defected, every nation engaged in the arms race assumed his fantastic claims were no hoax. Now a few are willing to have him blown away just to prevent us from getting the formula. Brolaika would do it for a price. My bet is that he's conned one or more governments into sponsoring him and his cutthroats to grab off what we've bought. Then he'll double-cross them and sell it to the highest bidder anyway. We've got to get to Ulrich first.

"I want you to be careful, Nick. Not that you're not a match for Brolaika, but under the circumstances, I'm withdrawing one of the restrictions I placed on you. Your holding back on Killmaster actions no longer applies. Nothing—absolutely nothing—should be allowed to stand in your way from picking up where Randolph was cut off. Nothing too flamboyant, of course. Keep it low-keyed, but pull out all the stops otherwise. Will you need some help?"

"I might. I'll let you know."

"I'll set something up on a standby basis. Meanwhile, feel free to call on anyone over there who is on the Langley payroll. Joe Corbin can identify them for you."

"Right now I need information more than help. I mentioned before that Professor Ulrich isn't here. Can you find out where he goes in Switzerland for some kind of medical care?"

"Data on Ulrich is a bit sketchy. It's available, I'm sure, but I've just been admitted into the magic circle and haven't had time to learn everything. I'll dig it out. His problem is no secret, though. That's one of the things that makes everyone here so anxious. Ulrich is suffering from sclerosing tanencephalitis, a degenerative brain disease. His is in an advanced stage and prognosis is not favorable. Which is why there is no time to lose. He's got to be located so we can obtain his formula. If it's only in his head, we can still lose it with his memory becoming unstable.

"You're right about treatments in Switzerland. He receives periodic injections of Isoprinosin administered under controlled clinical conditions. Inbetween, he takes a daily dose of a prescription drug to ward off minor epileptic spasms. He's that far along."

"Where in Switzerland? What hospital?" I asked impatiently.

"I don't know offhand. No problem on that, though. Since Langley's 'ghost squad' got him across the border, he's been a ward of our government. That means we're picking up the hospital tab. I'll find out which one."

"I'm going to Geneva," I announced.

"Stay at the Palais Royal Hotel so I'll know where to find you. Does Brolaika know you're in the game?"

"He knows me by sight now," I admitted. "He also knows—" I caught myself before blurting out that Brolaika knew my real name. Hawk wouldn't like that. It was a clue that might be used to discover that AXE was on the fringes of some nasty business festering in Paris. I went down the list of the dead: Randolph ... Fumiere ... Springer ... Otto ... all victims of Brolaika's savagery. Of them, only Springer knew my name until Brolaika found my passport on Springer. I didn't want to have to explain that unpleasant episode to Hawk. I started over again. "He also knows that I've been getting in his way. I'll watch out for him."

"Watch for him, yes, Nick. But remember, he doesn't work by himself. He'll have others looking for you now. I don't like the idea of you traveling alone. Join a crowd . . . you know the drill. Public transportation terminals can be traps, you know, so it might be best to use an automobile. I'd better arrange for the embassy to loan you an unmarked car with someone to go along to give you an extra pair of eyes."

I never knew Hawk to become so agitated that he injected himself into a problem as he was doing now. "Look, chief, let me handle it. I've already borrowed a personal car and I have someone in mind to take with me." My tone was just curt enough to be positive without being impertinent. It was a good note on which to terminate the conference.

Hawk closed with the words: "Good luck." For once his normally assertive voice seemed to lack punch and confidence.

TWELVE

I reached the embassy lobby just in time to see Kathy Frame and Frieda leaving by the front door. I caught up with them. "Did you get everything straightened out?" I asked. From the way Frieda stood close to Kathy, I could see that they had developed an immediate rapport.

Kathy's eyes moved up and down over my soiled clothes, but she made no remarks about my untidy appearance. "We'll have her fixed up in no time. Poor thing. She's frightened and absolutely exhausted. You must have subjected her to a terrifying experience."

I refrained from making a comment. Instead, I gestured toward the Lancia and said: "I have a car over here. May I take you somewhere?"

"Thanks, no. Leslie brought me." She tossed her head toward the opposite side of the parking lot. Standing next to a small Fiat, was a tall, broad-shouldered, angular individual wearing fitted slacks, a tailored coat and low-heeled shoes. A broad-brimmed hat over bobbed hair enhanced the illusion of masculinity. "Leslie's my roommate," Kathy added, beckoning to her friend.

Leslie came over with long, boyish strides. "Mr. Carter, this is Leslie Marsh," Kathy said. "She works down the hall from me in Central Files."

Leslie's was the baritone voice I'd heard over the phone. "Hi," she acknowledged the introduction. "As long as both of us were awake, we decided to come down together. It isn't always safe being out alone this time of night." Leslie passed Kathy an affectionate glance.

I understood Leslie's concern. Kathy looked dainty and feminine next to the deep-voiced sex-change candidate. In fact, I now understood a great deal more. I've seen paired off girls who lived together for reasons more intimate than sharing living expenses. I don't take sides on that issue. My only conclusion was that men didn't play a very important part in Kathy's life. Once more I was disappointed.

There was a question I wanted to ask Kathy that would give me more than one answer. "Remember I mentioned a young fellow who worked here as a courier up until a month ago or so?" Kathy nodded. "Did you get to know him at all?"

Leslie pulled a wry face and remained passive. Kathy answered. "No, I didn't—" Leslie's frown caused her to hesitate. "Well, you see—he was in and out so much—ah, we never had time to get acquainted. Joe Corbin knew him as well as anyone," she suggested.

Frieda's head fell against Kathy's side. Kathy looked down. "She's out on her feet. We'd better go."

* * *

Collette didn't wake up when I let myself into the apartment. My only reason for returning was to get my luggage so I could have a supply of clean clothes. Once inside the warm, quiet apartment, I knew I was going to stay. I couldn't keep going any longer. Like Frieda, I was about to fall asleep on my feet. I felt as if I had three layers of grime all over me. My hair smelled of smoke. My eyes still burned.

I was in the bathroom pulling my T-shirt over my head when the door pushed into my hip. Collette's disheveled head appeared around the edge of the door. Her eyes blinked against the light. Her pretty mouth was puckered with sleep. "Go back to bed," I said.

She gazed at my bare flanks sleepily, yawned kittenishly and squinted. "You will stay with me now?" she asked.

"I'm staying . . . only to sleep, that's all," I said wearily.

Her sleep pout turned to one of disappointment. "I'll wake you early," she promised. "I'm an early riser and I'll see that part of you is, too." She gave me a drowsy, impish grin.

"I'll set my clock so I'll be up at six-thirty." Collette thought it a teasing reply. It was no idle intention. I need only four hours sleep no matter how bushed I am. My brain has a built-in mechanism that never lets me oversleep. But I don't have the talent for staying awake indefinitely. A warm bath would put me to sleep instantly. I even found myself nodding and drifting off under a cool shower.

I slid into bed next to Collette as quietly as possible. She nestled her warm curves against my back. Inspiring though they were, my mind was programmed to turn everything off. I closed my eyes. Unconsciousness folded over me.

As suddenly as I had gone to sleep, I woke up. I looked at my wristwatch. Six twenty-eight. The eastern sky was a dirty, mother-of-pearl shade.

I eased out of bed. Collette was curled up, her blonde hair screening her small-featured face. I tiptoed about, finally finding my traveling bag tucked under the bed beside a varnished straw suitcase. I pulled out both. The lightweight one contained Collette's clothes.

The smell of brewing coffee reached Collette. She sat up. "You are dressed!" she said accusingly. Then she noticed that it was barely light outside. She fell back into her pillow. "It is still night," she complained. "What are you doing?"

I was using a kitchen knife to pry loose the lining inside my bag. I reached into the slit with two fingers and withdrew a well-worn British passport bearing my name. The photograph in it was not current, but my looks hadn't changed much in two years. The AXE paraphernalia section sees to it that the visa stamps on its pages are periodically renewed, but it was my fault that the photograph needed updating. I disregarded Collette's question. "Get up, sleepyhead. I'm going to take you away from all this. We're going to take a long drive in the country."

"Really? You mean it?"

"If you can be ready in five minutes."

She sprang from the bed and dashed into the bathroom. Except for the chain with the key around her neck, she was needle-naked. An instant later she came out again. She ran up to me and kissed me on the cheek. She gathered up her straw suitcase and took it with her. "Bring me *café au lait,* please, when it is ready. I need ten minutes."

We were on our way in fifteen. The warming sun was just lifting over the apartment building roofs. I took Route N-5 going south out of the city. Forty-five minutes later we were in Fountainebleau.

While a filling station attendant serviced the Lancia, Collette and I watched from across the street where we sat at a sidewalk cafe having coffee and croissants. She was one of those people who took a long time to wake up. She listened with half an ear, showing little interest in my greatly modified explanation for being delayed the night before, or how I had come by Randolph's car. She showed no further interest in his prolonged absence. Collette was a simple soul who took things as they came on a day-to-day basis.

When the station attendant waved to indicate the car was ready, I leaned toward Collette and whispered, "How would you like to go all the way to Geneva? We could be there for lunch."

That woke her up. She grabbed my hand. "I would love that, *mon cheri*. It is mos' convenient. I am to return in a few days, regardless. My plastic surgeon mus' review his handiwork. I will be grateful that you take me with you. You will see."

From Fountainebleau I took connecting Route N-51 to get on the Autoroute du Soleil. We rolled along at a moderate rate. Collette first sat upright, taking in the striking autumn colors with childlike pleasure as we passed through central France's rich agricultural region with its famous vineyards, orchards and treed pastures. She prattled about herself, her childhood in Brittany, convent school in Rennes, days as a department store clerk in Paris and her ambitions to become a mannequin. It was my turn to listen with less than full attention.

Long before reaching Dijon, Collette exhibited her feline qualities once more. She adjusted the bucket seat, curled up in it and dozed. I turned on the radio, keeping the volume low. I scanned the dial until I picked up a Paris-based all news station. The signal faded as we came to the section of the highway that wound through valleys in the rolling country around Auxerre and before the police report was broadcast. I never learned if my anonymous call that led police to the brutally-murdered Randolph also produced a search for his missing automobile.

After leaving Lyons the terrain turned mountainous. The road became a tortuous, twisting path with sharp switchbacks and breathtaking views. Collette was fascinated, never having made the trip by automobile before. She slid forward in her seat as we descended the straight, downhill stretch of road leading to the Swiss lakeside village of Nyon. She was delighted and excited by the spectacular panorama.

The prominent, braless contours under Collette's thin nylon blouse were examined more closely than either her passport or mine when we crossed the French border. The mouth of the middle-aged Swiss customs officer fell open when Collette answered his routine question why she wanted to enter Switzerland with a candid, boastful reply. Thanks to Collette, my substitute

British passport received only a cursory inspection.

For more than two centuries Switzerland has remained neutral in a world beset with wars. This is due partly to the fact that the rugged Alps, which cover half the country, are uninviting as a battleground. At the same time, the snow-covered mountain slopes have turned the country into a winter vacation mecca. The modern marble-and-glass façade of the Palais Royal Hotel looked out across the eastern tip of Lake Geneva with towering Mount Blanc in the background.

The reception clerk's eyebrows hardly moved when he noticed that the names on the pair of passports I gave him did not match. He studied mine longer than necessary, then excused himself. A moment later he returned and handed me a folded note. "For you, from our switchboard," he said simply. On it was written my name and a telephone number preceded by the international area code for Paris. The number meant nothing to me. The memo carried no indication that the call was important or urgent. Even if it had, I'd take my time about calling back. I wanted to think about it first.

The bellboy looked disapprovingly at the frayed straw suitcase when he picked it up. His attitude changed when he saw that it belonged to Collette. He couldn't keep his eyes off of her during the elevator ride to our eighth-floor room. I gave him a bigger tip than he deserved. While Collette unpacked her few things and hung them in the double closet which was part of the dressing alcove next to the bathroom, I studied the telephone number on the switchboard memo once again.

The thing that worried me was that someone could be curious enough about my whereabouts to call every hotel in Geneva hoping to find me registered at one of them. I've used that technique myself. A strong possibility was Brolaika. I had to assume that Brolaika's backers were feeding him as much—and probably more—information as I was getting from Hawk. It was reasonable to believe he knew of Ulrich's illness and the professor's periodic trips to the Geneva clinic. Frieda had admitted to him that Ulrich was gone from Paris. As I had done, Brolaika would conclude that the logical place to pick up the trail was Switzerland. He could be well ahead of me. One way for him to short-circuit me was to find out if I had arrived in Geneva and where I was holed up.

When Collette went into the bathroom, I used the phone. It took an inordinately long time for the call to be put through. That in itself didn't sit too well with me. The delay could be caused by taking time to shunt the connection through a recorder. So it was totally unexpected when the first words I heard were: "Hello, Mr. Carter. This is Kathy Frame. I have some information for you."

"Is Frieda okay?"

"She's fine. That's not why I called. I was asked to give you the name of a hospital. It's the Suisse Institut d'Psychologue located at Karlstrasse 37."

"Thanks. That helps a lot."

"I'm afraid it doesn't, Mr Carter. You see, I've instructed the staff there not to release any information. Well, I didn't make the rule myself. It's policy handed down from . . . from back home, you know."

"Who steered you onto me?"

"A friend of yours in Washington who called here this morning. It's too bad I didn't know your plans last night—but then you didn't know that I was in a position to help, either."

"If I'm blocked from getting what I need from the Institut you're still not helping," I reminded her.

She sounded uncertain. "Oh, dear. I had no idea how complicated these things become. I was only involved with the personnel aspects and monitoring payments at first. It's gotten a little beyond routine now."

"It's anything but," I agreed. "How do I go about finding what I want to know?" I was growing impatient.

"This may surprise you, but I've already tried. Your boss explained how important it was. But the one person who is authorized to talk to me—the patient's doctor—is out of town and can't be reached. He isn't expected back at the clinic before tomorrow morning."

I swore to myself, damning the obstacles in my way. "Will you be at this number if I call back?" I asked in a barely controlled voice.

"Yes. Anytime. I'm always here or at home."

I could picture her at home with Leslie. I was teed off at the situation just enough to needle her. "I'll bet your diary is crammed with exciting entries."

I had to wait a moment for her answer. "I stopped keeping a diary when I was fourteen." I could guess what she started doing instead. "I prefer to keep my private life private," she said icily. I didn't expect her to be so sensitive. I needed friends, not more enemies. I was on the verge of apologizing for my imprudence when her voice continued. "Please respect that, Mr. Carter," she said pointedly. "And now I think everything has been said that needs to be. I don't have anything to give you. You must be patient. There is nothing for you to do but wait."

A moment after I had hung up the phone, the bathroom door opened. Collette came out wearing a towel, sarong-fashion. For the rest of the day we behaved like honeymooners. I called a halt to Collette's insatiable demands long enough to have room service bring dinner for two just before the kitchen closed for the night.

After dinner, Collette took a warm bath, then crawled back into bed. "I will sleep awhile," she sighed contentedly.

The shower I took failed to curb my building restlessness. I dressed, gathered up my soiled clothing and carted them downstairs to the valet. They would be ready by seven in the morning. I made a tour of the hotel's ground level, then went outside and made a circuit of the building, examining it from all sides. There was no real purpose behind my actions; I do it more from habit than anything else.

My watch showed a few minutes before six when I was awakened by the sound of a key being fitted into the door. I slid out of bed and ran across the carpeted floor. I listened and then relaxed. I turned the locking latch on the inside door panel that opened on the valet closet. My dry-cleaned suit hung in a cellophane bag. The laundry was in a blue cardboard shirt box.

I was in the dining room drinking my second cup of coffee after an excellent breakfast when the maitre d' brought a telephone to my table. Kathy Frame was on the other end. "Good morning, Mr. Carter." Her voice was businesslike. "I hope I'm not bothering you. I know it's quite early."

"You wouldn't be calling if it weren't important. Did you get in touch with the doctor?"

"Yes. He makes hospital rounds first thing every morning. I've just talked to him. He saw his special patient three days ago. The man is not well, but he refuses to be admitted for more intensive care. I think you know why. If he stays too long in one place—" She knew I was aware of the consequences.

"So he's trying to keep out of sight. Any chance he'll contact you, Kathy?"

She didn't chide me for using her first name. "There's no reason why he would. He doesn't know that I exist. There is something else you might want to follow up on, though. The gentleman was given five prescriptions for the sustaining drug he needs. One of them was filled yesterday in Davos."

"What would he be doing there?" My question was rhetorical.

"Traveling?" suggested Kathy. "It's a couple of hundred miles in the direction we don't want him to go. You know, the way his mind is—" She left unspoken the obvious conclusion.

"How do you know the prescription was filled yesterday?"

"The pharmacist was uncertain of the dosage.

He called the hospital to clarify what was written on the prescription slip. I learned the call came from Vellar's Apothecary in Davos, but there's no point in phoning back. Swiss law prohibits pharmacists from releasing information about dispensing controlled medications.

"I guess I'll be heading east, too. Would you mind passing that on to my supervisor?"

"I'm to call him as soon as I finish talking to you. He thinks very highly of you, by the way. Before I say goodbye, Mr. Carter, I'd like to say I'm sorry I got a little huffy yesterday."

"I pushed you into it," I admitted. "My friends call me Nick."

"All right," she brightened. "Be careful, Nick."

I went back upstairs to pack and let Collette know that we were parting company. She was dressed and using the telephone. The conversation concerned an appointment for a checkup.

"But Nicky, darling, what will I do all by myself?" she asked when I told her I had to leave for a day or two. She wouldn't be alone very long unless she wanted it that way. "Take me with you," she coaxed. "I do not see my doctor until next Friday. Please. I will not interfere. If I do, you send me back. I will bring myself back in time for the appointment."

I rejected the idea until I remembered that Hawk would expect me to follow his pointed recommendation that a double pair of eyes was good insurance. I didn't anticipate any trouble on the way to Davos. Once there, it could be a different story. "All right, you can come along," I agreed and braced myself.

Collette came flying across the room. Her arms went around me. She showered my face with kisses.

The drive around Lake Geneva and then eastward through the Rhone Valley was a constant delight to Collette. The scenery changed continuously, blending rural charm with formidable peaks. Rustic villages with a clustering of brown-roofed cottages dotted narrow lateral valleys between forested slopes. Isolated chalets perched in unbelievable nooks or on rocky crags accessible only by winding, single-lane roads.

The streets of Davos were snow packed when we arrived. The Vellar Apothecary was next to Trauffer's souvenir shop on Davosplatz. I left Collette there while I went into the drug store. The smiling youth manning the pharmacist's window wore a white, choke-collar work tunic. He looked young enough to be an apprentice. An older man behind him who was talking into a telephone was the one I would have preferred to question. I asked anyway. The prompt reply was unexpected. "Why, yes. I remember the Ulrich prescription very well. We don't get many calls for that particular medication."

"I've come all the way from Geneva to see the old man about an important business matter. Did he leave a local address?"

The answer was a frown. "That prescription wasn't brought in by an old man. Two men came here, neither one old. Mr. Vellar served them, but I helped. A tall man with his arm in a sling had the prescription, but he also bought cotton, antiseptic and gauze. For his friend, perhaps. He had a bandaged face. We see lots of that—bruises and contusions from falls on the ski slopes."

It had to be Brolaika and his trigger-happy cohort whose face had been cut by chipped foundation stone from the Rue Hendrix house. Hawk said that Ulrich's failing health and his need for periodic treatment was common knowledge. In Paris, Frieda had revealed to Brolaika that the old man was gone and was due to return to Switzerland. Brolaika had reasoned exactly as I had—and had reached Ulrich first. Ulrich, with a supply of prescriptions in his pocket, must have walked out of the Geneva clinic and right into the waiting arms of one of Brolaika's men.

"Do you have any idea how I might find Professor Ulrich?"

"The automobile the men used came from the Dragner Schloss near Klosters. I know the cars—they are big English sedans. They are part of the package offered to private parties who rent out the old stone chalet for skiing vacations."

I tried to conceal any show of inner excitement. The senior pharmacist had hung up the telephone and was coming up to take part in the discussion. I hastily thanked the young man and went to the front of the store. At the door I turned to look back. The druggist was engaged in earnest, serious conversation with his flustered trainee. It looked as though he was being given a lesson in Swiss law regarding prescription privacy.

I found Collette in the rear of Trauffer's shop examining the intricate lace work of a tablecloth. I moved up behind her and used an intimate and inviting whisper to ask: "Do you ski?"

She spun around, beaming. "I love it! But I am far from expert."

"We will see," I promised. "Ettinger's Sport Shop can outfit us to look like old hands." Collette clutched my arm as we walked through the falling snow. She hung on to keep her balance while trying to catch large snowflakes in her mouth.

While the rented ski rack and skis were being mounted on the Lancia, Collette and I were fitted out with a complete assortment of ski togs and accessories. It was easy to see why she aspired to become a mannequin. Her lovely figure gave highlights to the canary yellow three-piece outfit that had a formfitting tailored vest that zipped to pants and included a matching, lightweight parka. I chose a dark blue padded jacket to go over dark blue coveralls. The color was picked for practical reasons I had in mind. One being that next to the eye-catching Collette, no one would take notice of me. As it was, with gloves, knit caps, walking boots, and wide lens goggles, both of us would blend well into the mainstream of winter resort visitors.

The store clerk was very helpful. He pointed to a display board on which current ski conditions were posted. "Klosters has a forty-inch base on most slopes. That's a lot for so early in the season, which is not always a good thing. The snow is very dry and hasn't packed down. It makes for unstable conditions. You must be careful to avoid avalanche-prone places. Keep to posted areas where the patrols have checked and you will have no trouble." He lowered his voice. "You, *mein*

Herr, I can tell you know skiing, but your pretty little companion . . . keep a close watch over her. Don't let her wander off, but then—" he ogled Collette admiringly, "—I imagine you don't let her get too far from you at any time."

I passed him a knowing grin. "Perhaps you know of accommodations in Klosters that offer more privacy than a hotel? We don't like lobbies or elevators filled with people."

His right eye winked. "Of course. You want the Reinnach Haus, an excellent hotel with private cottages on its grounds. Here, take my card," He scribbled a name on the back. "See Hans Sweigart; he is my cousin who works there. This early in the season and in midweek there should be no difficulty . . . if you don't mind, perhaps, offering an appropriate finder's fee."

The quaint Alpine village of Klosters nestles at the base of a narrow valley formed by the Parsenn mountains. The Reinnach Haus sat back from the main street at the end of a short, curving drive. The snug, two-room cottages behind it had rear walls partially imbedded in a gentle slope that quickly became a steeper incline. I stood behind Collette and peered over her shoulder as she looked out through the side window. Children enrolled in the hotel's ski school were receiving instruction on a beginner's slope. In the background a gondola moved up along a cable. We watched it until it became obscured by the gently falling snow.

Collette turned from the window and bent to examine herself in a dressing table mirror. She made a wry face as she fluffed her hair. That gave me the opening I needed to enable me to get away by myself. "I'd just as soon skip the skiing until the snow stops," I began as a preamble. "Would you like to visit the hotel beauty shop?"

She couldn't resist the offer. "Oh, I mus'," she agreed, pulling at her hair. "I will look real nice for you. But do you mind?"

"You go along. I'll look around the village," I replied, voicing the intention that had prompted my apparent generosity.

The kiss she gave me before she tripped out of the cottage door still tingled my lips when I set out by myself. In twenty minutes I knew every street, alley and hidden doorway in Klosters. It was a typical compact Swiss village. I stopped in one of the freshly painted little shops and purchased a used Leica and a new 135mm, eight-power telephoto lens. For my purposes, it was as good as a pair of binoculars, and far less noticeable. On the way to the edge of town, I stopped in the central telephone office and sent a wire to Kathy Frame. The important part of the otherwise meaningless message was the originating point of Klosters which indicated my present location.

The sun was penetrating the thinning clouds when I got back on the street. The snow had stopped. The last building on the street was the village church. I hoped I appeared to be a camera-toting tourist photographing the Grison coat of arms decorating the clock tower when in reality I was looking over the terrain and the high-perched Dragner chalet some three miles distant.

The main road going east was fairly level. It cut through a three-foot carpet of snow although deeper drifts had accumulated on the uphill side. A single lane access road forked off to lead to the large stone house anchored a good five hundred feet upslope from the valley base. Much deeper drifts along that road had been plowed through to keep the drive free. In one place, the snowpack on the uphill side of the road had collapsed and needed clearing again. The unstable snowpack was a dangerous nuisance to road maintenance crews.

I elevated the telephoto lens and focused on the gray stone chalet. It was a formidable, blocky-looking mansion which accounted for it being classified as a *"schloss"* or castle. I could make out the distinctive radiator of a Bentley sedan whose nose jutted out through an archway that appeared to lead to an inner courtyard. The sight supported the Davos pharmacist's contention that Ulrich's prescription had been picked up by a guest at the Dragner chalet. In the few minutes I concentrated on the fortresslike structure, I saw three men, identifiable as such by size and clothing. Their features were too indistinct to be recognizable.

What I saw and what I couldn't see made me decide I needed a closer look. I returned to the Reinnach Haus and left a message in the cottage for Collette. It told her I would be back in time to take her to dinner and dancing later.

I looked forward to my first use of skis in months. Despite the warning to keep only to posted areas, my planned course required me to ignore that basic safety rule. It started at the top of the Weissfluhjock slope, reached by two sets of cable cars. From that peak, the normal run back to Klosters is over six miles with a difference in altitude of almost five thousand feet. Mine was an exhilarating series of wedelns and Arlberg turns to the halfway point. From there I broke trail cross country through heavily wooded slopes.

As the sun lowered and shadows lengthened, I hurried to reach a vantage point above and near the Dragner chalet. In my haste, I grew careless. Twice I had to race ahead of loose, tumbling snow like a surfer riding before a churning wave.

It was then that I realized that getting back safely was more important than making a detailed reconnaisance of Brolaika's refuge. I skied past it in the fast-falling dusk, noting the general layout. From the number of lights burning behind many windows of the three-level citadel, it appeared that Brolaika was making full use of the chalet. The results of my cursory surveillance were disappointing, but I gained an appreciation of the dangers of open-space skiing between Dragner Haus and Klosters.

Collette was not in the cottage. She had found my note; it was in the wastebasket. I was in the bathroom shaving when she returned. I looked into the mirror to see her standing behind me. "I had to go back for a bottle of nail polish," she explained. I smiled and nodded my approval of her hair style. She pirouetted to show off her dress. It was an inexpensive off-the-rack model. The way she filled it more than compensated for its lack of originality.

Collette sat at the dressing table working on her nails. I realized that it was time for me to send her away. I would miss her, but didn't want her around when my final confrontation with Brolaika occurred. That would take place as soon as I could get word to Hawk that I was ready to accept his offer of help; this was no longer a job for one man.

I completed dressing for dinner, making sure that my jacket—specially tailored to accommodate the bulge of my gun holster—was properly draped over it. I drew the pistol and slipped out the magazine to check the cartridge alignment in it. Collette glanced up and saw me in her mirror. "Does it bother you that I carry a gun?" I asked, wondering why she had never mentioned it.

"I do not find that unusual," she answered. "You are Jacques' friend. I presume that is because both of you do the same work. I know his job—carrying very important government papers—involves some risk. He had a gun. It follows then, that you, too, would have a weapon." Her loose logic brought her to a simple conclusion.

A light knock came at the door. Collette jumped up. "I will get it," she said, reaching out for the knob.

"Wait!" I cried out, but I was too late.

She had turned the knob, releasing the latch. The door flew open, pitching Collette backwards into me. I was trying to shove the magazine back up into the pistol butt when we collided. I didn't succeed. A hairy hand at the end of a long arm thrust the nozzle of an aerosol can in my face.

The spray was icy cold and stung my eyes, blinding me. Some went up my nose and reached my throat. I gasped involuntarily. My lungs drew in the biting vapor. The insidious gas turned my knees to rubber.

I felt myself going down. There was no way to stop it.

I fell, but I never reached bottom.

THIRTEEN

I opened my eyes and tried to bring the world back into focus. The first dim shapes that took form appeared to be twin trunks of tall trees whose bark had been peeled off leaving smooth white stalks exposed. I blinked my eyes a couple of times and tried again.

This time I oriented myself. I was flat on my back on the floor in the rear seat of a moving automobile. The bare tree trunks became Collette's long, shapely legs. On either side of hers were trouser-clad male legs which seemed to end at the knees. I couldn't see beyond the edge of the seat on which the trio sat.

I grunted and propped myself up on an elbow. One of the male legs slammed a big, boot-clad foot down on my shoulder, stamping me back against the carpeted floorboards. "Just relax, Carter. We haven't much farther to go," I was told. The voice was clipped, deep-toned and laced with a strong

Slavic accent. I was too groggy to worry about the exact geographic placement.

The car was moving along a winding road. Concrete, I guessed, from the smoothness of the ride. Through the side window above and opposite me I could see high-piled banks of snow.

The car slowed, then made a hard turn into another curving, uphill road. From my prone position I saw the peaked roofline of the Dragner chalet come into view. It disappeared when the driver passed through a stone archway into a courtyard. The automobile made a wide, sweeping turn and came to a stop.

I was the last to leave the car. Rough hands jerked me up on my wobbly legs and pointed me toward heavy oaken doors leading into the mini-castle. Collette, her hands tied behind her, was flanked by two burly men. The one with the bandaged face propelled her roughly into the chalet. She managed to twist around to look at me before being pushed through the door. The expression on her face was a mixture of bewilderment and stark, helpless fear.

The third man, the driver of the car, was a broad-faced peasant type with a brow so narrow that the peak of his chauffeur's cap concealed his forehead completely. He manhandled me with the strength of a full-grown grizzly bear. I was so weak and confused that a ten-year-old midget could have controlled me with ease. I was prodded through a narrow passageway to another heavy door. It opened on another small, inner courtyard.

I strained to implant the layout of the building and grounds in my barely receptive brain. The main cobblestoned court was roughly square in shape. It served mainly as an enclosed parking area for two British sedans identical to the one that had brought us here. Next I was thrust through a dim passageway and into what appeared to be a wide, walk-through closet. Among other things, it contained a rack for skis and ski poles. On one wall was a long row of wooden pegs from which jackets, raincoats and some parkalike garments hung.

Brolaika was standing at the far end of the room lighting up one of his thin, dark cigars. It was my first time to see him clearly in full light. His eyes were close-set, beady and intense. He had a high forehead accentuated by a receding hairline. His most unusual feature was a total lack of eyelashes and eyebrows. It gave his strange, elongated face an obscenely naked, reptilian appearance that I found singularly repulsive. "You shan't be here too long," he advised in a flat, nasal tone. "We intend to interrogate the woman to learn what she has been told unless you wish to tell us first. I believe, however, that she will be easier to persuade than you."

I heard only half of his threatening words, but the meaning came through clearly enough. "She knows nothing," I replied. "Give me a chance to gather myself together and I'll explain everything."

"Do not take me for a fool, Mr. Carter," Brolaika sneered. "She knows a great deal, as would any slut who gets involved with a Yankee who interferes with legitimate efforts to recapture a defector."

"You call your actions legitimate?" I shot back. "I know your kind, Brolaika. A ruthless mercenary

... a bounty hunter willing to take blood money from anyone willing to shut their eyes to what you do." I baited him intentionally, hoping he would react and blurt out something that would help me.

I should have known better. Brolaika drew on his freshly lit cigar reflectively. He was a stern professional not likely to be drawn out. Still, he couldn't resist saying: "So you know who I am. Congratulations, Mr. Carter. Then you also know it is useless to resist. You may want to point that out to your friend."

He didn't give my still-fuzzy mind time to formulate a reply. He waved an imperious dismissal with his cigar-holding hand. "Put him in the turret room," he ordered the driver who gripped me with hands like a closed vise. Brolaika's arrogant hand motion was a degrading rejection indicating that anything I might say would have no influence on his planned course of action.

I was shoved through large, well-furnished rooms to a central stairway. Brolaika and his squad of goons were not planning to stay long. None of the protective dust covers placed over the furniture had been removed. Large fireplaces in the rooms showed no signs of having been used recently. Whatever Brolaika was up to didn't involve any prolonged activity.

My legs felt like lead by the time I got to the top of the long, curving stairway. I used the balustrade running along an upper balcony for support until I reached the hallway pointed out to me. At its far end another switchback stairway continued upward to a third floor. I climbed it wearily.

The ceilings were lower on the third floor. The

slopeheaded chauffeur prodded me forward until we were somewhere near the outer wall of the chalet. He pointed down another short corridor that ended at another heavy oaken door. The ugly atavist uttered a guttural sound and bobbed his neanderthal head toward it. He possessed enough intelligence to be cautious despite my still-uncoordinated movements. He remained behind me in the hallway and drew out a long barrelled Schmeiser automatic. He used it as a magic wand to emphasize his mute directions, and I obeyed. The insipid grin he wore revealed heavy, uneven teeth. He was one I'd be careful about arguing with, even if our positions were reversed.

I backed into the solid door and tried the handle. The door was locked. I turned back to Slopehead and turned my palms outward in a questioning gesture. His grin turned sheepish, then faded quickly. A frown darkened his broad face. He reached into a pocket and tossed a large key toward me. It unlocked the door.

I entered the room, leaving the key in the lock. A moment later the door was shut behind me. The key turned metallically in the bulky brass lock securely riveted to the thick door.

The room was circular. Bright moonlight filtered in through a single, head-high window. It took a moment for my eyes to accommodate to the reduced light in the room. Before I could see anything clearly in the fifteen foot diameter enclosure, I first sensed the cold. The room was unheated. Instinctively I wrapped my arms around me and hunched my shoulders.

I made out a bundle of blankets piled up against

the wall. I rushed over to it and found a man cocooned among the tattered quilts.

At first I thought he was dead. His wide open eyes stared unblinking straight ahead of him from a sallow, lined face so cadaverous that a week-old corpse would look the picture of health by comparison. The sunken cheeks were covered with a waxy, parchment-texture skin. His lips were nearly colorless: they carried a slight tinge of blue from the frigid cold.

He lifted his head slowly and with obvious effort. He gazed blankly into my face. "You've come," he gasped. "I knew you'd come." He reached out a trembling hand that was skeletal-thin and heavily veined. His long fingers, possibly crippled by arthritis, were curled like talons.

"Professor Ulrich?"

The man's gnarled hand wrapped around my wrist. "Thank you, thank you," he said. "I knew you would not fail me." He seemed to gain strength, as if contact with another human transferred energy into his frail body. The old man was incapable of clear thinking. It took no feat of clairvoyance to realize he had me confused with Randolph.

"You have come to tell me—" Ulrich stopped, as if trying to remember what message he expected.

I had none. No message—just a lot of questions which Ulrich was in no shape to answer. If he were, I'd have a worthwhile source of information. As it was, I was confronted with another dead end. No wonder Brolaika had no hesitancy in putting me in the same celllike room with Ulrich. I was going to learn nothing from the feeble scientist while he was in such an unfunctional condition. Nevertheless, I had to try.

"I'll tell you what I can," I promised, kneeling down with my head close to his. "What is it you want to know?"

"Greta—my daughter—Greta. You have found her? She is safe?" His clawlike grip on my forearm tightened.

I had no answer to give him, but I might learn more from his lead. "Greta?" I said.

The old man pulled himself up to a sitting position and leaned against me. "You promised. It was agreed. She was to be kept safe—taken secretly from Hungary and protected." He stopped, catching his breath. "I must know before I tell you—tell you—where—where—" He fell back, exhausted from the effort.

"Where what?" I urged.

Ulrich rewarded me with a dull, vacant stare.

"Where? You were saying where?" I suggested to jog his faltering mind.

"Where is Greta?" he responded. "You have her safe," his voice rambled. "My beautiful child—we will go see her."

"You mean Frieda?" I questioned, raising my voice so he would hear.

"Frieda?" His eyes narrowed while his mind groped. "No. She is with Otto. It is Greta—yes, Greta who needs—"

Ulrich was physically too weak to continue. More than that, his thoughts drifted, seemingly lucid one moment, then senseless the next. Whatever was left of it was so wrapped up with concern for his daughter that all other thoughts were either distorted or shut out entirely.

Ulrich closed his eyes and once more he looked dead. His eyeballs under wafer-thin eyelids threaded with tiny blue veins looked like ping pong balls bulging out from their skulllike sockets. I detached his bony fingers from my arm and laid him back. I drew the soiled blankets around his narrow shoulders, then began pacing around the room and swinging my arms vigorously to keep warm.

On my second circuit of the room, I almost ran into the door which was flung open unexpectedly just as I approached it. Slopehead stood in the doorway backed up by Brolaika who held the machine pistol this time. The burly, dimwitted giant next to him moved toward me upon receiving his leader's signal. With surprising speed for such a big man, Slopehead snatched my right wrist and cranked it around until he held me in a painful arm lock.

They marched me down a flight of stairs and along a hallway until we came to a warm bedroom. Collette lay on the double bed, spread-eagled and completely naked. Her ripped off clothing was scattered about. Collette was gagged. From the welts and bruises on her body, the gag was the only reason I hadn't heard her screams.

I surged forward, blinded by uncontrollable rage. A tighter twist of my arm by Slopehead stopped me.

Brolaika stepped over to the bed where I could see him. "You see, Mr. Carter, the girl has been uncooperative. She is a strong little bitch, but she now faints too often. You must persuade her that she suffers needlessly. Tell her you want her to talk to us."

Collette had been subjected to more defiling torture than just the cruel bruises marring her smooth white skin. Only a savage pervert would permit anyone to endure such foul, inhuman punishment. "What do you expect of her?" I demanded. "I told you she knows nothing."

Brolaika glared at me, judging the truth of my words. He crooked the small finger of his free hand and used its over-long fingernail as a pick to dislodge something caught between his teeth. "I'll accept that," he said finally. "So observe the woman as an example of what is in store for you. She is nothing—a whore not worth bothering about. She has talked, but said little. Perhaps we have extracted from her everything of value she knows. We have no further use of her."

"You can't just let her die."

"You will be cooperative then, Mr. Carter? You will tell us how to recover that which was stolen by the traitors?"

Brolaika's words barely registered. I was enveloped in pity for Collette, fearing that if she didn't receive attention very soon, it would be too late. "Release her!" I demanded.

In shouting, I gathered strength. A writhing leap and tumble freed me from Slopehead's grasp. The move also put me within kicking distance of the one other man who was already in the room when I was brought in. I needed to get past him to reach Brolaika.

My leg lashed out. The heel of my shoe rammed into the surprised man's groin. He almost fell on top of me as his knees folded, dropping him to the floor where he groveled and groaned. I rolled away, but not before Slopehead drove a kick of his own into my back. It launched me toward the bed I was trying to reach.

"Carter!!" Brolaika's strident voice hit me like a sledge. I faltered from its impact, but the shot I expected to hear or the bullet it preceded never reached me. "Look up! This way," Brolaika ordered. Still no shot.

I rose to my knees and glanced across the bed. Brolaika was holding the muzzle of the Schmeiser two inches from Collette's temple where perspiration-soaked hair was pasted to her head. Her big eyes were wide with terror and her smashed lips clenched the blood-flecked gag tearing at the corners of her mouth.

I got to my feet and stepped back, defeated. The triumphant leer on Brolaika's face made my stomach churn. I had made a mistake and he reveled in it. So intent was my attention focused on Brolaika that I barely felt the crush of Slopehead's renewed hold around my body.

To my amazement, Brolaika thumbed off the safety of the pistol he held and took a half-step backward. I couldn't believe he was serious until he pierced me with an insane, icy look that chilled my blood.

"DON'T!!" I screamed, but my protest was drowned out by the explosion that filled the room. Collette's head snapped sideways. Bone, blood and pasty gray matter spewed across the bed and splattered on the floor next to it.

The nauseous, gory sight had a dramatic effect upon Slopehead. He gasped, sucking in a huge breath. I felt an easing of pressure in his arms locked around me. I stamped down hard on his foot so I could break loose. He didn't let go completely. We gyrated together wildly, whirling around unsteadily like two euphoric gorillas in a grotesque mating dance.

I was facing the bedroom door when I finally broke loose.

My freedom came too late.

The sound of the shot that blew away Collette was like a magnet to two of Brolaika's hench men who heard it. They kicked the door open in my face. For a breathless moment no one moved. A frontal attack was my only out.

As I gathered myself for the charge, both men before me whipped out odd-looking handguns and fired them pointblank. I felt a sharp prick in the thick pectoral muscle above my left nipple.

I looked down. A small, folding-fin dart stuck straight out from my chest. The fast-acting tranquilizer ejected from its hollow-needle nose was already making my vision fuzzy.

My head grew heavy. It remained in a bent-down position as my legs folded under me and dropped me onto the floor.

Once more I fell into the bottomless pit of absolute darkness.

FOURTEEN

Sight returned as if someone was removing layers of opaque film in front of me one sheet at a time. Slowly, a scraggly haired head took on definite form. Ulrich was bent over me, trying to lift my swimming head from a folded blanket placed under it.

"I—I'm all right," I said. The voice didn't sound like mine.

Ulrich held his hand in front of my face. If he expected me to count fingers, he'd have to wait. My eyes weren't up to seeing anything but vague shapes. The old man kneeling next to me was persistent. He kept nudging my arm. "This is what they used on you," he said.

I strained to focus my eyes. His swollen-jointed fingers held a hollow-pointed, two-inch dart gingerly by its tail fins. I reached out to take it. The professor withdrew it from my reach. "Careful. It's still loaded. This is one I found lodged in the shoulder padding of your jacket. The other was stuck in your chest." Ulrich guided my fingers to avoid the needle-sharp point as he transferred the tranquilizing dart to my possession. "It may help you escape," he said.

My mind had cleared enough to understand and endorse the idea. Brolaika's frisking had stripped me of both pistol and knife. Pierre, the miniature bomb, had been overlooked and still nestled in my groin. "What time is it?" I groaned. The dungeonlike room was filled with gray light.

"Just daybreak," Ulrich answered after a slight hesitation.

"We've got to get ourselves out of here," I decided, propping myself up groggily on one elbow. The floor seemed to wobble. Ulrich steadied me.

"No," he disagreed. "Just you. I would never make it."

He was right. But he also appeared stronger. His speech was more controlled. Unlike before, he now acted as though he knew exactly what we were talking about.

I tested him. "You remember me, don't you. We talked last night."

"Yes. Was it last night? We talked of my family, and you had seen Frieda, you said."

"And Otto, too," I added. "I was with both of them in Paris. They are in good hands." I figured that wasn't too far from the truth.

Ulrich stretched his pale lips into a weak smile. "I am glad," he said. "And the French girl? She left the hospital, of course."

Now he's testing me, I thought. Only Randolph would know that Collette had had cosmetic surgery. But why would Randolph talk to Ulrich about his girl friend, or the old man be interested? I had to keep his confidence. "She recovered rapidly," I replied, having to steel my voice to keep the emotion out of it. "She was back in Paris three days ago." I got to my knees and bundled the unsteady man in the blanket he had folded into a pillow for me. "Are you feeling better, now?"

"Oh, yes. They gave me my medication. During the night...when they examined you. It helps, you know. For a while. It wears off too quickly now. They say I have built up a tolerance for it...but I know better. Soon it will do me no good." He studied my face intently during the long speech. "Why did you come here?" he asked at the end.

"To find you."

"Why? You have what you want."

He could be referring to the REAM sample he had prepared and left with Otto, but I knew there was more. I didn't want to introduce more details into the conversation than his mind could handle. I kept it simple. "Otto gave me the bottle from the wine cellar. We still don't have the rest of it."

"You have the key and Greta is waiting. You don't need me anymore." He bent forward suddenly, clamping his hands to his temples. His face grimaced with pain.

"Wait," I said, scrambling to my unsteady feet. The room couldn't be bugged, but someone could be eavesdropping at the door. It was made of thick oak set in the frame to leave a good half-inch gap at the bottom. A chill draft wafted through it.

By laying flat and pressing one cheek against the floor, I would be able to peer under the door and see into the hallway. I didn't want anyone opening the door into my face, so I took one of the thin blankets and wedged it tightly between the latch side of the door and the frame. It acted like weather stripping, blocking some of the incoming air. A stronger draft whistled past my face when I knelt down and looked through the gap.

No one was standing close to the door. I could see a pair of boots and legs up to knee-height backed against the far wall of the corridor opposite the door. I guessed that beetle-browed Slopehead was back on duty.

Bent over with the blood rushing to my head, a lot of things began to fall into place. It was not an idle or wandering mind that had sparked Ulrich's question about Collette. I snapped my head around to look at him. He was hunched over, swaying from side to side. I crawled to him and spoke in a low voice.

"You gave the key to Collette when you were in Geneva at the same time." I made it sound more like a statement than a question. I hoped I was getting through to him.

"Yes. Collette. That was her name. That's how you planned it. I gave the name to the florist to write on the envelope. Instead of a card, I placed the key inside. Just as you instructed. It was a clever plan—sending her to the hospital—then my sending the flowers. We did not have to see each other. Both of us were safe." His last words were a groan.

I was afraid I was going to lose him. He was beginning to tremble noticeably, and not from the cold. "Safe," I picked up. "A safe deposit box key." I said as much to myself as Ulrich.

His chin began to quiver. "Yes. My notes. Safe —there—in the bank." He rolled away from me, clutching his sides. "Go! Leave me!" he wailed. His voice rose in a piercing plea. Then he let out a screech that filled the circular room. He continued to roll closer to the door. "Leave me!" he wailed again. His legs jerked spasmodically as the convulsion approached.

Someone pounded on the door. "What's wrong in there?" Slopehead's gruff voice called out. Ulrich let loose another pitiful, gargling moan. Spittle ran out the edges of his mouth.

A metallic grating sounded as a key was inserted in the door lock and turned. "Stand back," Slopehead ordered. The latch on the outside rattled. The blanket wedge prevented the door from swinging in. "What's going on?" the gruff voice questioned. "Let me in!"

"It's the old man," I called out. "He's having a fit." He was. His frail body jerked and trembled. His eyes rolled back in his head. "The door's stuck. Push hard!" I yelled.

I was ready to take advantage of the windfall opportunity. I had the tail end of the door blanket in one hand. My other hand was balled up into a fist. Projecting from it was the fast-acting tranquilizer dart, point forward, sticking out like a miniature dagger.

Nothing happened.

Then I heard another voice—Brolaika's oily voice—growing in volume along with his approaching footsteps. I had to change my plan with the change in odds against me.

I listened until the low-speaking voices merged

just beyond the door. I jerked back my hand holding the blanket. It peeled out of the door crack without a sound.

I snatched open the door and charged out into the hall. Surprise was my ally. I exploded into the pair, catching both offguard. My hands were a blur as they moved. I jabbed the paralyzing dart into Brolaika's chest harder than necessary. The stiff edge of my other hand, moving faster than a swung axe and just as deadly, lashed out at the startled Slopehead. It smashed into his throat hard enough to rupture the thyroid cartilage of his voice box and send him reeling. His slim-barreled Schmeiser automatic pistol flew from his grasp.

Brolaika remained immobile. His head dipped. His lizardlike eyes stared at the protruding dart. As I watched, his left leg bent and he went down on that knee before he toppled over helplessly. His hard, piercing eyes, glaring with an inner, insane light, never left my face until the lashless lids closed over them.

I knelt beside Slopehead. His eyes were open, but glazed over. It no longer made any difference that he would never talk again. He had suffocated in seconds from a crushed windpipe.

I returned to Ulrich. He lay quiet, but he wasn't dead. The convulsion had raged through him and left him weak, almost comatose. His breathing was shallow, but regular. I did what I could by wrapping blankets around him to keep him warm.

Both Brolaika and Slopehead were dressed for out-of-doors. Brolaika was the taller man...more my size. I rolled him on his side and began removing his down-filled jacket. His limpness got in the way. The last tug to finally free the padded jacket from his left arm sent a shiny object skittering across the floor. I recognized it at once as the gold chain Collette had worn around her neck. The steel key was still attached.

I knew now why Brolaika and Slopehead were dressed to go outside. There was no reason for them to remain at the chalet any longer. The dying Ulrich was no good to them, even if they took him the few remaining miles across the border. Whatever Brolaika had gotten out of Collette was enough to make him aware or suspect that the key she wore was valuable. She surely would have admitted as freely and innocently to Brolaika as she had to me how she had acquired the unusual gift...thinking it a present from a lover who would explain its purpose later. I had to give credit to Randolph. He had held out against Brolaika long enough to die before he could reveal that his unsuspecting French paramour held the master clue to his deadly puzzle.

I jammed the necklace and key into my pants pocket. I got into Brolaika's jacket as I ran down the hallway to retrieve Slopehead's weapon. From where I picked it up, Brolaika's head was only twelve feet away. I can hole a postage stamp from that distance. I'd use two shots to make doubly sure.

But that would make noise. It was possible that Brolaika and Slopehead were not the last two still in the chalet.

I turned the Schmeiser around, gripping it by the barrel to use it tomahawk-fashion on Brolaika's fiendish brains. After two strides toward him, I had my mind changed for me.

A questioning voice echoed up the stairwell behind me. I heard footsteps climbing the stairs at the end of the hallway. They stopped before the man's head had risen above floor level. He had paused at the landing. The second time his voice carried loudly down the vaulted corridor.

I had two choices. If I ducked into the turret room, he wouldn't see me, but he couldn't miss the two prone figures. The other choice was the bold approach: I might fool him into thinking I was Brolaika long enough to gain the advantage.

When in doubt, I take the offensive.

I ran toward the stairs, keeping close to the corridor wall. The voice from the landing called out again. This time it had a no-nonsense tone that clearly expected an answer. The man was alert and cautious.

Each of us saw the other at the same instant...and he was ready. The sound of his shot in the narrow stairwell was amplified a dozen times. His bullet, fired more from reflex than intention, went wide. It ploughed a deep scratch along the corridor wall. His second shot went through the ceiling above him because he was already falling backward from a 9 mm. Schmeiser slug through his forehead.

I scrambled down the stairs, vaulting over the body. The ground level floor was dark. Heavy, closed drapes held back most of the early morning light. The chalet would become a death trap for me if I didn't get out before Brolaika's men reacted to the gunfire. I wished I knew how many there were. I hoped to avoid all of them. The best chance for a clear escape lay in reaching the outer court where the automobiles were parked. I can hot-wire most cars in under fifteen seconds.

Voices were calling back and forth. They seemed to be concentrated just where I wanted to go. I skirted two sofas and a coffee table to get to a large window looking out into the cobblestoned court. Three Bentleys were there, along with four men. All wore warm, outer clothing. All were armed. Two had Sten guns slung over their shoulders.

The quartet was holding a hurried conference. The one obviously in charge and receiving rapt attention was Brolaika's top gun. One side of his face was covered by a bandage. I doubted he was going to stand by and let me walk away, regardless of whether Brolaika was around to endorse his decision or not. He had good reason to hold a personal grudge against me.

The four men separated. The two with the Sten guns remained with the automobiles. They took up protected positions behind the hoods of the two Bentleys, ready to cut down anyone attempting to enter the courtyard.

The bottom fell out of my plan to steal a car.

I heard an outside door open quietly, then close. I eased behind the heavy drape, gun at the ready. Two shadowy figures came into the room and spread apart quickly. I could almost touch the back of the one standing closest to me.

"I hear something," a hoarse whisper said. The man spoke German.

"Where?" A second German voice.

"Sounds like upstairs. Listen."

I listened too; it could be the wind. Or the turret

room door swinging back and forth in the draft. I fancied it to be Ulrich's raspy breathing. Heightened senses and a little imagination can generate a lot of strange effects.

"Hear it?"

"*Ja*. It's upstairs all right. I hear no voices, though. *Herr* Brolaika came in to bring out Hans and Sergeiv."

"I heard three shots. Could be the end of the old man and the American."

"Then what's holding us up. Maybe we'd better go back and wait with Stefan and Gunter."

"It's quiet for too long. We'd better check."

"Upstairs?"

"Of course, *dummkopf*. You take the second floor. I'll go to the top."

"Turn on the stairway light."

I figured I had no more than a minute before the alarm sounded. In a minute, I hoped to be well on my way.

Enough light from the stairwell reached the walk-through closet containing the ski equipment for me to see what I was doing. The Schmeiser tucked into my waistband kept jabbing me in the ribs as I tried on boots. Finding a pair of skis whose step-in bindings could be adjusted to the ski boots took the longest time.

I cradled both skis and ski poles under one arm and slipped out through the side door, keeping in a low crouch. The piled-high snow embankment lining the cleared driveway offered concealment from the men in the courtyard while I worked with the ski bindings. It never occurred to me that someone might look down from an upper window. The shout startled me and alerted the courtyard guards.

The bindings weren't set tight, but I leaped up anyway, dug my poles into the snow and pushed off. I used the double pole stride technique to put distance behind me. The first useful fall was fifty yards away. I reached it and dropped rapidly into a gully as the first Sten gun burst ripped the early morning silence. The few lights still burning in the village at the bottom of the hill glowed weakly in the brightening sunrise. They looked to be a hundred miles away instead of three. The weather was clear and not as cold as I expected. A warming chinook wind blew down the slope. . .bad news for skiers.

I plunged recklessly down into the depression. I had no intention of stopping, but I did. My right boot slipped out of its binding. The loose ski shot out ahead of me. I dove after it awkwardly. Luckily, I recaptured it.

My fingers worked rapidly to secure the ski bindings properly so I could continue. It took time. When I finished I looked back. I was not the only skier on the slope. Stefan and Gunter were launching themselves in my wake.

Their tactic became apparent at once. Both set a course to remain uphill from me. The lead man called back an order to his companion. With his face turned away I couldn't hear him, but I heard the reply. "*Ja*, Gunter, I understand."

I understood too. The pair intended to force me to use the steepest part of the slope where tricky moguls abounded. A spill on the rough, bobbing terrain would stop me long enough again for them to bring their shoulder-slung weapons to bear.

Within the first two hundred yards Gunter

proved himself to be the better man of the two. He quickly developed catch-up speed despite the rolling, dipping terrain. Neither of us could use our weapons. Bouncing and flying at breakneck speed, every ounce of skill was needed just to stay on our feet.

Gunter closed the gap between us. For a space of a hundred yards, we raced head-to-head with Gunter slowly narrowing the lateral distance that separated us. He was intent upon spilling me so that Stefan, just behind, could stop, set himself and riddle me with bullets from his Sten gun.

Gunter's face was mostly hidden behind his goggles, but it was close enough for me to see his triumphant grin. He was sure of himself. He had a right to be.

With nothing to lose, I took a long chance. Instead of making a last, desperate French avalement to turn away, I reversed the obvious escape maneuver and executed an uphill tip roll to cross in front of him. Too late, the surprised Gunter twisted his body and lifted his ski pole to parry the one I lunged out with like a thrusting pike. The hard steel tip of my pole pierced his clothing and buried itself in his belly just below the sternum.

Releasing my improvised lance, the impaled Gunter tumbled forward, his skis riding over the backs of mine. I lost my balance, went down on one knee, but caught myself with the remaining ski pole I'd hung onto. Gunter rolled head over skis. The shoveling effect started a snow slide. A large shelf of snow rumbled down the slope, but spread out and subsided before it became a true avalanche.

I got underway again with Stefan now closer to

my heels. Both of us were running almost parallel to the dug-out access road leading up to the Dragner chalet. One of the Bentleys was racing down it toward the village. Another two-pronged pursuit was developing.

Closer to the access road, the mountainside was smoother, but the slope steeper. The present snow conditions make it a dangerous track for skiers. Small clouts of snow cascaded downhill constantly in the wake of my passage over it. Stefan knew the signs. He remained fifteen yards upslope and slightly behind. He knew as well as I that the weight of the two men concentrated over a weak spot in the snow pack could collapse it and trap both of us in a major slide.

I flattened my fall line, slowing my speed. Stefan did the same but edged closer. He must have thought it strange that I shoved my hand deep down into the waistband of my trousers. It came up holding Pierre. While basically a gas bomb, Pierre's detonator explodes with the force of a hand grenade. My plan to use it solely on Stefan changed when I saw the pursuing Bentley rounding a curve only a short distance behind.

I went into a downhill racing stance, picking up speed again and moving closer to the edge of the access road. The going was treacherous—so much so that Stefan hesitated using his extra elevation to speed up as well.

He had nerve, all right. He executed a sharp christie turn to convert his altitude into additional speed. I pressed the fuse activator on Pierre and tossed it uphill away from me. The muffled sound of the bomb exploding where it was buried in the snow was nothing like the cry of terror Stefan gave as the snow dropped underneath him. The snowpack peeled away, sloughing like a falling glacier wall. Tons and tons of thundering snow swept down the slope. Stefan's skis cruciformed above his rag-doll body just before it disappeared behind a solid white screen.

I swung wide, heading uphill for safety. The snow base trembled underfoot, but held. Not so behind me where a moving cloud of roiling snow marked the downhill progress of the avalanche. I could barely see the access road directly in the path of the expanding snowslide.

The driver of the Bentley had heard the tremendous release of energy. He stopped the car. The two occupants jumped out. They knew what was coming. They had no chance to run. There was no place for them to go. They were trapped within the high-walled snow trench.

The avalanche surged over the road, obliterating it from sight. The halted automobile was lifted and hurtled sideways when the solid deluge struck. The big car was tossed, toylike, then swept away. Along with the men who had been in it, the battered automobile would rest at the bottom of the valley in an icy grave until next spring.

FIFTEEN

I rounded the rear corner of the hotel cottage and snowplowed to a stop. The stout woman who performed the housekeeping chores was sweeping a dusting of snow from the walk. She recognized me. Tucking the broom under one arm, she came over and unlocked the cottage door for me as I bent down to detach my skis. "I'll be checking out shortly," I informed her. I spoke to her back because she was looking inside the cottage. She couldn't miss seeing that the bed had not been used during the night. She stepped aside, allowing me to sit on the door stoop to unbuckle the ski boots. "I'll be out in half an hour."

I intended to be gone in half that time. I cleaned myself up and got into fresh clothes. My feet appreciated getting into proper-fitting walking shoes. I threw Collette's belongings into her bag and repacked mine, keeping out Brolaika's jacket. I called the bell captain for a baggage handler. While he carted luggage and ski equipment to the Lancia parked in the garage, I walked in the brisk morning air to the main hotel building.

The cashier told me the road east of town was temporarily blocked by an avalanche. I thanked her and accepted my receipt and the two passports which Collette and I had relinquished and left with the hotel for safekeeping at the time we had registered. The waiting bellboy held open the door leading to the garage with one hand while palming the tip I gave him with the other.

The garage attendant was standing next to the Lancia. He pointed to a rear tire. It was nearly flat. The cap was missing from the valve stem. It could have dropped off, but its absence suggested to me that someone had purposely let air out of the tire. I certainly couldn't drive on it.

"I have a hand pump," the overalled attendant offered, turning away.

It irked me to think he was using a dodge to solicit a bigger tip. By the time he had returned with the pump, I had the bags in the car. The garage man worked agonizingly slowly, making a big deal of a simple task. I could have done it faster.

When enough air had finally been added to make the tire useful, he dug into his pocket and held out the missing valve stem cap for me to see. He wore a grin on his face.

"You've got a hell of a lot of nerve," I growled.

"She asked me to do it...to keep you here." The hand holding the valve cap pointed behind me.

I spun around.

Kathy Frame was walking toward me. She wore a satisfied smile, too. She was attractively dressed in knee-high leather boots, a gray A-line skirt, cowl-neck knit sweater and a hip-length fur jacket. She wore clothes well. Her pretty blue-green eyes flashed with barely concealed humor when she saw my surprised reaction. "Well, aren't you pleased to see me?"

"More than you know," I replied.

"You're leaving?"

"I'm late now," I said meaningfully. "My business here is finished."

"Would you mind giving a girl a lift?" She dipped into her shoulder bag for money to pay off her overalled accomplice. He accepted with a thankful bow and retreated. "I'm sorry, Nick. I had to resort to chicanery in order to contact you without being too obvious."

"You shouldn't be here at all."

"That isn't what that nice Mr. Hawk told me. As soon as I mentioned where you were, he asked me to come here and set up what he called a base. You aren't telling him what's going on often enough to suit him. He said you had a tendency to understate the situation and were inclined to write your own ticket. He told me that, ordinarily, he wouldn't mind. In this case, though, the outcome is too crucial to give you a completely free hand. I know the problem.

"Mr. Hawk told me quite a bit. He must be a very important man. My boss hardly whimpered when he turned me loose so I could help out. He even had me driven to the airport so I could catch the first plane to Zurich. I'm to notify Mr. Hawk at once if you need any assistance."

The details of what had occurred in the past twelve hours were unimportant now. All Hawk really would want to know is that one vital segment of the chain leading to Ulrich's treasure had been restored. I had the safe deposit key. Ulrich's daughter was the only remaining element. Though he hadn't said so, it was fairly obvious to me that Greta Ulrich was the only person with privileged access to a bank vault containing the safe deposit box and its extraordinary contents.

"There's nothing more to do here," I explained. "I'm pretty close to the end of the trail. I'll be there when I see Professor Ulrich's daughter. You mentioned her. She's being kept in Geneva by your people, isn't she?"

"Yes, but I don't know any details. I said I had the job of clearing the vouchers connected with the Ulrich case. I didn't know at the time why our government was making such a special fuss over some Hungarian refugees. As I recall, the daugher is established with a cover of being an intensive care patient in Ste. Moreaux Hospital on Rue de Lausanne."

"I'd like to leave right away. There are reasons why we shouldn't waste any time."

"You're in danger?"

"Not the way you think. I could be inconvenienced if I wait too long."

Kathy studied my face. "I'm ready. I haven't anything with me but an overnight case. I'll be back with it in five minutes."

I drove as fast as the road conditions and winding curves would permit. Patches of snow and ice on shaded portions of the highway made high speed driving treacherous. Kathy reached into her shoulder bag. "You might want this," she said, handing me my United States passport. "Inspector Du Brau sent it to the embassy. An honest city sanitation worker turned it in along with Ralph Springer's. The inspector is upset that you left Paris without leaving a forwarding address. What *were* you up to that night just before you brought Frieda to the embassy? The inspector has lodged a rather serious protest through the Foreign Office hinting that you might know something about an illicit drug ring?"

"He's confusing me with someone else." I had my eye on the rear-view mirror. An automobile with familiar protuberances atop its roof trailed us. It kept disappearing from view as we rounded curves, but used the short straight stretches to close up. I pressed harder on the accelerator, then drew my foot back. There was no way I could avoid the police. The Lancia could outrun an ordinary cop car, but it couldn't burrow under a road block set up to stop me. When the blue lights on the car's roof began blinking, I pulled off onto the berm.

The uniformed policeman was polite. Having noted the Lancia's license plate, he spoke French. He didn't ask to see my driver's permit. "If you please, *monsieur*, you must turn around and go back to Klosters."

"Are you arresting me?"

"*Mais non, monsieur*. It is about the avalanche. Some questions. We understand that you may have witnessed it while skiing very early this morning. You can aid the investigation. You see, a body has been found. Also a skier. It is for that we must detain you."

I took my time leading the police vehicle back to

Klosters. I used it to coach Kathy on how to play the upcoming scene and to jam the Schmeiser pistol up under the dashboard. Kathy entangled it in the electrical wiring there to hold it in place. I gave her the safe deposit box key. "Get back to Geneva. Take a room at the old Hotel D'Angleterre. If I don't show before six tomorrow morning, call Hawk and tell him you need help. He'll take it from there."

The police station was in the basement of the hundred-year-old municipal building. The pink-faced, baldheaded sergeant in charge had acquired a lot of facts...some of them true. A surprising number of villagers had seen the avalance in its final stages. Some had caught a glimpse of a skier racing away to safety. The housekeeping maid employed by the Reinnach Haus volunteered that I had returned to the cottage on skis right after the avalanche had occurred.

He stopped there and turned to Kathy. He told her that she was courting charges by using trickery to hitchhike a ride with me. As a prelude to dismissing her, he started to caution her about accepting rides from strangers. He didn't get to finish. The sergeant was called from his office. He stood outside the left-opened door talking with a young blond man wearing a Ski Patrol patch on his windbreaker. After a moment, the sergeant reached out and closed the door.

Minutes passed in silence. Then an officer came in and said we would have to vacate the sergeant's office. Kathy was told she could leave. She did without saying goodbye or looking back. I was taken to a room occupied by a silent, older man assigned to clerical duties.

I sat there for nearly two hours. I smoked the last of my cigarettes. The officer who had evicted us from the sergeant's office looked in on me twice. Each time he apologized for my having to wait. Another serious police matter had developed. The sergeant had called in a special investigating team from the canton government in Chur. A member of the ski patrol had reached the Dragner chalet and came back with distressing news. He didn't elaborate. He didn't have to. I suddenly needed some fresh air. "Would it be all right if I went out to my car for cigarettes?" I asked.

"Why, of course," the officer replied pleasantly. "You will find it in the back lot."

I found it, all right. It was impounded, stuck behind a padlocked chain link fence. I decided I could do without the cigarettes. I didn't want the lot attendant poking around the map case compartment looking for cigarettes and coming up with the hidden Schmeiser.

I returned to the clerk's cubby-hole office and waited again. He left for lunch. When no one came in to replace him, I got up and opened the door. A cluster of men, uniformed and in business suits, stood at the foot of the stairs. The pink-cheeked sergeant was among them. He spied me and walked over quickly. "Oh, Mr. Carter. I am so sorry. Really, I forgot about you. This other matter—" he let it trail off. "You see—" he gestured to the group of men gathered at the stairs. All had the look of law enforcement types about them. "I got so involved—" he kept apologizing. "Please forgive me. I should have released you. The avalanche is of small concern now. Your car is—"

"I know where it is," I interrupted, eager to be gone.

"But wait!" the sergeant said. "I'm afraid I have erred again. The impound lot. . .the man in charge is with the detail I sent up—We are a small police force, you know. Ah, I have it. I am leaving now to go there myself. I will send him back immediately."

"That's kind of you. I don't mind waiting," I lied, playing the innocent. "I'll have lunch and then come back." I was honest about the lunch part. My gnawing stomach begged for food.

I followed the half dozen men up the stairs and out into the bright light of early afternoon. They got into cars at the curb and headed in the direction of the chalet. I stood watching, calculating how best to cope with a fast-developing dilemma. I was deep in thought when a hand locked on my arm. It belonged to Kathy Frame. She had her overnight case with her.

"What are you doing here?" I asked sharply. "I told you to clear out."

"I'm going! I either take a bus leaving in an hour for Lucerne where I catch a Swissair flight that puts me in Geneva at nine o'clock tonight, or take the night train leaving at six-twenty. I have to wait somewhere, so I picked a spot across the street, hoping you'd be released before I had to leave."

"We shouldn't be seen together," I said roughly while I started moving her along the sidewalk. "We're only casual acquaintances, remember?" I couldn't keep the irritation out of my voice.

"Like you and the French girl were?" Kathy said accusingly.

"Keep quiet!" I ordered, leading her down a narrow side street and into a small, family-run restaurant. "I'll tell you about it while we have lunch."

I chose a table in the rear and seated Kathy with her back to the door. I sat opposite her so I could see the street through the large front window. She began on me as soon as we had ordered. "You didn't tell me you had a girl with you!" Her tone was critical. I couldn't figure why it mattered to her, unless every heterosexual relationship was that distasteful to her. If I hadn't concluded differently about her attitudes, it sounded as if she was jealous.

"The girl supplied the key I gave you. Without it —without her—we'd be back to square one. She'll never know how important she was to what we're doing. She's dead now."

"Dead?" Kathy said unbelievingly. "How?" There was interest rather than fear in her glistening eyes. She had rather remarkable eyes. She was, in fact, wasting a great deal of her loveliness by denying it a normal outlet. Under different circumstances—much different circumstances—I could really enjoy her company.

The arrival of a pipkin of Kirsch-laced Gruyere cheese fondue saved me from answering. We started spearing cubes of coarse bread with long-handled forks and dipping them into the bubbling pot. I glanced up idly to look beyond Kathy. A familiar face peered at me through the street window. I didn't want to be seen, but the man recognized me. He smiled a greeting, then his face became serious.

It was Hans, the helpful assistant manager who had established Collette and myself in the cozy hotel cottage.

"Don't look around," I warned Kathy as I jumped up and left her.

"Ah, there you are, *Herr* Carter. I was worried about you and your lovely lady." He glanced in Kathy's direction.

"Worried?"

"Well, when I learned you didn't occupy the cottage last night, and then this terrible business at the chalet—" he stopped when he saw the puzzlement on my face. "Oh, you don't know? The murders in the Dragner chalet. The victims are being brought down now. Two men dead and a pretty blonde woman. It crossed my mind—you know—with the empty cottage. But there is more. An old man near death and another unconscious from an apparent drug overdose have been taken to the infirmary. It's the worst crime the village has ever had. I just learned of it from one of the ski patrol who discovered the bodies."

Hans was a gossip. He could hardly wait to leave me and carry his gruesome news elsewhere. I went back to Kathy. "The dam's broken and I could be drowned in the flood," I told her. I explained how circumstances were closing in on me. It wouldn't take long for someone to suspect that the mutilated female body equated to the blonde girl who, along with me, was absent from the cottage the entire night before I checked out so hastily this morning. Linking that with other events of the past twenty-four hours would pinpoint me as a common denominator. "It won't do me any good now to regain use of the Lancia," I went on. "The occupants of every automobile, bus and train leaving here are going to be checked in order to find me. We have to separate before you get boxed in, too."

Kathy's brow knitted in thought. "It's too bad we can't box you out," she muttered softly.

"What was that?"

She smiled weakly. "A silly, wishful thought. I was thinking of boxing you up and shipping you out. . .on the train."

It was an idea. . .certainly not brilliant. . .and totally impossible. It couldn't be done. Then it hit me. Why not? There were boxes of sorts on a night train. All I needed was a way to slip into one without being seen. With Kathy's help, I might be able to do it. I hunched over the table and spoke rapidly. As I laid out the plan before asking Kathy if she was willing to take the risk, her eyes sparkled with understanding and eagerness.

"Yes. I want to," she asserted. "We'll do it, I know we can. But, Nick—" She reached out with her hand and touched my face. "Be careful. Be *very* careful."

SIXTEEN

From the Bahnhof opposite the Baderwiesse Hotel in Klosters, the Swiss Federal Railway reaches Davos after climbing slowly through stately pine forests and crossing a lofty bridge spanning the Landquart River. Only then does the train start picking up speed as it descends through Wolfgang, another skiing resort, and continues in a generally straight path to the base of the Davos Valley.

The Landquart bridge is approximately seven miles from Klosters, but it seemed like twenty to me. It was all uphill. Increasing cold and darkness made the last two miles of trudging on railroad ties and crushed rock seem endless. I got to the bridge a good half hour before the train would arrive. It was a long, miserable wait. I had time to think.

On balance, I was confident so far. After Kathy had told me she had slipped the Schmeiser into her shoulder bag when she was permitted to get her overnight case from the impounded Lancia, I allotted myself a maximum of one hour to do some essential shopping. I took the gun and all the money Kathy could spare and added it to my reserve kept under the zippered lining of my leather trouser belt.

I spent it freely, going rapidly from shop to shop. I didn't want to remain too long or make too many purchases in any one place. The ski gloves and face mask I was wearing came from the same store where I bought a small rucksack. It now contained some hardware, a twenty-foot length of nylon climber's rope, the loaded Schmeiser and two tools: a ball pien hammer and a tempered steel punch.

The hardest part after that was keeping out of sight until it was time to get the last-minute information Kathy was to supply. At five-thirty I called the public phone located in the Bahnhof waiting room. She answered on the first ring. "What can you tell me?" I asked.

"Well, like you figured, there's tight security down here. Three men are running things. A railroad trainmaster, a uniformed policeman and a man in a business suit who seems to be in charge. A plainsclothes man, I'd guess. It's like going through customs. You have to have a ticket just to get in the passenger waiting room today. Once inside, you stay inside. It looks like we're going to be personally escorted aboard the train. I'll be in compartment B-7, a very comfortable box. That's in the last car of the train until it gets to Davos where other sleeper cars are hooked on. The train leaves at ten minutes to eight."

I had plenty of time to get to the Landquart bridge. Trouble was, in my haste to leave Klosters,

I'd started too early. I knew the uphill hike would keep me warm, which is why I passed up the chance to buy a set of thermal underwear. Now, huddled beside the bridge abutment, wet and getting cold, I wished I hadn't.

The train, holding to Swiss railroad tradition, was on schedule. The moment I saw the creeping locomotive headlight, I crawled up the icy-cold steel structure of the trestle bridge and wrapped myself around a horizontal I-beam while the train approached. A chill wind buffeted me. My cold fingers began to cramp. I thought the train was moving dreadfully slow while I waited. When it came time to drop down onto the roof of the moving railroad car, I thought differently.

It worked out almost the way I had visualized it. Almost. I've gone through some wild acrobatics in my time and take pride in keeping in shape; this effort would prove once and for all whether my coordination and judgement were up to a unique challenge. The vertical distance was no more than eight feet. My forward launch speed had to match that of the train exactly. If too slow, I'd tumble backward. If my forward motion was too great, I'd somersault head over heels. With each car that passed under me, I made practice forward surges to get the rhythm. When the last one rolled by, I leaped.

I didn't think the crosswind would have much effect. I was wrong. Instead of landing squarely atop the flat roof, I touched down with a slight lateral movement. I went down on both knees and a shoulder, momentarily off balance. To keep from rolling, I threw out both arms and extended my legs, ending up flat and spread eagle on the cold metal roof. There was nothing to cling to—only gravity pressing my one hundred eighty-five pounds onto the inhospitable surface kept me from sliding overboard.

Wind blasted my ears. I silently thanked the Swiss railroad engineers for building and maintaining a smooth roadbed. The car beneath me swayed very little. But the train, having crested the pass, began to pick up speed.

I crawled closer to the left side of the roof. A row of yellow lights shining out from the sleeping car windows raced alongside the train. The pale rectangles undulated as they moved across the rolling, snow-clad terrain adjacent to the roadbed. One of the light squares was supposed to flash off and on after the bridge was crossed. That was the signal Kathy would give to pinpoint the location of her compartment and indicate it was safe for me to join her.

The string of lights gleaming on the snow burned steadily. I grew colder. The temperature was dropping. The wind chill factor created by the train's movement had a marked effect. I clung as best I could to the sloping metal roof of the car. As the downhill speed of the train increased, so did my chances of losing my grip and sliding off. What was keeping Kathy from flashing her compartment light? Surely she had heard the distinctive rumble of the train as it crossed the trestle. She was watching and waiting for it.

Something must have gone awry. I stared at the line of lights blurring past. Their rippling against the snow produced a hypnotic effect. Along with the cold and the wind, I felt myself becoming numb. I closed my eyes, then snapped them open.

One of the squares of light disappeared. Then flashed on again. It continued . . . on . . . off . . . on . . . off. I knew where compartment B-7 was. I belly-crawled the fifteen feet to be poised over it.

My nearly-frozen hands could barely feel the metal shaft of the sharp-pointed, steel punch grasped in my fist. My first hammer blow set the point. Three more produced a definite hole in the roof. Another three and the hole size was large enough to accommodate the heavy-duty hook I dug out from the bottom of my rucksack. Attached to it was a swiveled pulley. I threaded one end of the nylon climber's rope through it, then set the hook in the punched hole. I tested its purchase by tugging hard on both strands of the rope strung through the pulley. The hook held.

The first use I made of the anchored rope was as a safety line. Hanging onto it, I leaned far over the edge of the roof and looked in the window. Kathy was standing next to the closed compartment door with her hand on the light switch. Her expression showed amazement then relief when she saw my upside-down head.

I reversed myself, winding the double rope under thigh and over opposite shoulder, then rappelled over the roof's edge feet first. Despite gloves, my hands were so cold that my grip on the ropes was uncertain. My entire body was shaking. My teeth chattered. These were definite symptoms of approaching hypothermia. I had to get inside before I ended up hanging outside Kathy's window like a frozen, tangled-string marionette.

I hung, swaying helpless, while Kathy struggled with the window. It was typical of European railcars. Their windows are equipped with leather or tapestry straps attached to the lower part of the pane. To open a window, the sash must first be lifted to disengage the sill, after which the window can be lowered into a slotted recess. Only a frosted pane separated me from the warm, lighted, box-shaped compartment. The window resisted Kathy's efforts. She tugged and strained.

Dangling by one hand, I applied the other to the stubborn window. Kathy's face grimaced with effort. Between us, we succeeded. The window snapped loose and dropped out of sight. I pushed back into the wind, then swung feet first into the compartment. Kathy grabbed my legs. I twisted around and released my hold on the ropes. I fell to the floor, but got to my knees quickly. I snatched up a single rope and pulled it in, hand-over-hand. It ran through the pulley anchored atop the car and fell loose. I threw the rest of the rope out the window and pulled up on its lift strap to shut out the whistling, bitterly-cold wind.

The window jammed, leaving a four-inch gap at the top. That was of small consequence at the moment. I was aboard, out of the cold and assured of a safe ride until reaching Geneva.

Kathy was beaming. "I was so worried. The train was checked after it got underway. Two policemen just left me. They went over the compartment with a fine-toothed comb. They even made the conductor use his special tool to unlock the upper berth for them—as if anyone could hide up there!"

Kathy's bed was made up, the berth above it closed and locked again. Kathy was prepared for sleep. Under a filmy, knee-length robe she wore practical, brushed-nylon pajamas. The tips of her breasts showed the effect of the sudden blast of cold air upon them. Her nipples were prominently erect. Until now, I hadn't been particularly interested in her femininity. I saw that she was lush and amazingly well-proportioned. She became conscious of my frank, admiring examination. "You're all right, aren't you?" Her tone was one of concern.

"Ye-yess," I replied. "Just c=cold."

I snatched a blanket from her bed. I squeezed into the tiny lavatory and ran water into the stainless steel wash basin. I soaked my hands, bringing life back into dormant fingers. Only then could I unbutton my shirt and shed my wet clothes. I got down to my skivvies and wrapped the blanket around me.

I opened the narrow toilet door and stepped out. Kathy was at the window, trying to close it. "Here, let me," I said.

"It's stuck," she explained needlessly. A stream of frigid outside air flowed through the wide gap.

We stood shoulder to shoulder working to lift the window. It was hopelessly jammed in the partly-opened position. Kathy and I bumped and pushed against each other in our efforts. I became very aware of her soft body coming in contact with mine. "It's no use," Kathy admitted. Her teeth were chattering now. "W-What s-s-should we do?"

"Get in your berth and cover up!" I ordered. She

got out of the way. I took one of the two bed pillows from her and forced it into the window gap. It helped, but fell short of plugging the opening by some eight inches on one side. The hole admitted more cold air than the compartment heater could offset.

Kathy lay snuggled under the sheet and the remaining blanket. She was shivering. I paced back and forth to keep warm. It was a losing battle. "You're go-going to w-w-wear yourself out," she stuttered with clicking teeth. "C-c-come here. We'll ha-have to hu-huddle together. Share both blankets." She sat up.

I joined her. It was a very inefficient and awkward arrangement. Awkward in the sense that a man and a woman—even though obliged to press themselves together for warmth with only a thin layer of material separating contact—cannot remain long without becoming extremely conscious of the intimacy. Kathy continued to shiver. I wasn't regaining much body heat.

"This isn't going to work," I decided finally.

"N-n-no," she agreed. "We've got t-t-to—" She couldn't finish the sentence. She stood up and made a shoving gesture with both hands. I discarded my blanket and crawled under the sheet, then slid back against the bulkhead. Kathy hurriedly spread my blanket out over me, then layered hers on top of it. She got into the bed, nestling her backside in the curve formed by my stomach and drawn-up knees. She pulled the sheet and blanket up under her chin. She trembled and shook, her teeth still chattering. Her foot touched mine. It was icy cold.

The train rumbled on. Warmth began to spread through me. Kathy's shivering subsided. Our combined body heat trapped under the blankets warmed both of us. The sleeping car rocked with a gentle, sensuous, back-and-forth motion. It caused Kathy's buttocks to rub and jostle against my loins repeatedly. I began to have feelings that were in no way connected with recovering from the bone-chilling cold. My perturbation was increased by having my face buried in Kathy's soft, scented red hair.

I wondered if Kathy had fallen asleep. If so, she was not wholly relaxed. Her breathing was abnormally shallow and rapid. I hated to disturb her, but my arms were in an uncomfortable position stretched out straight at my sides. I had to move them.

The most natural thing was for me to put one around her. I did, slowly and gently. And I got a surprise. My wrist slid over the rise of her breast. The tip was erect and hard again. Not from the cold this time. Kathy let out a tiny gasp at my touch and her buttocks jerked involuntarily.

I couldn't believe it. She was sexually aroused. I tugged with the arm that reached around her. She turned in the narrow bed to face me. Our noses were an inch apart. Her lips were parted, her breath coming fast. Her eyes looked into mine with willing, burning expectation.

I slid the hand reaching around her down to her hip to draw her close. She trembled with anticipation. Then she pulled back sharply and rolled out of bed. Barefoot, she ran to the locked compartment door. I feared that she had been so repelled by having awakened and found herself aroused by a man that she was going to flee into the corridor and blow the whole thing.

It was my fault. I told her so. "Please, Kathy, I'm sorry. I got carried away." She was clutching her robe collar up around her throat. "It's just that you're so beautiful, I forgot that—I mean—you know—that you can do without men."

"What makes you think that?" she asked with raised eyebrows.

"It's pretty obvious, isn't it?" I countered. "You —and Leslie."

"Leslie?" Her eyebrows changed direction.

"Yes. Your lesbian lover, Leslie Marsh."

"Oh, Nick!" Her voice dropped with disappointment. Her hand moved up to the light switch and turned it off. A pool of pale moonlight streamed through the window. She stepped into it. Cold as it was, she removed her robe and tossed it aside. "You're very mistaken about me, Nick," she said softly. The two pieces of her pajamas dropped to the floor. I gaped at her moonlit loveliness as she moved toward me. "And now, I'm going to show you just how wrong you are."

The sky was gray when I awoke. The train had slowed as it approached the outskirts of Geneva. Kathy was asleep, a serene, gratified look on her face. I marveled at her lovemaking that ranged from fiery passion to extreme tenderness. Her mouth was slack with fulfillment, her breathing deep and even.

I crawled over Kathy. She awakened. Her hands tried to detain me. "Get moving, lazybones," I said. "We're vacating this cozy love nest in five minutes."

"You'll find us another?" she called after me as I disappeared into the compact lavatory to wash and dress.

Kathy was pulling her sweater over her head when I came out. We exchanged places. I removed the pillow-plug from the window and lowered it all the way. I stuck my head out into a thin, pearly fog. It blanketed the lake shore a quarter mile away. The train wheels clicked frequently passing over frogs and switches. Parallel tracks grew in number from two to six. Strings of boxcars occupied sections of siding.

I moved over to the lavatory door. "Hurry!" I whispered. "Cornavin Station, the end of the line, is just ahead. We're creeping through the freight yards now. Time to bail out."

Kathy joined me. She sat on the bed to pull on her boots. "I'll go first," I said, grabbing up my rucksack. "Then I'll trot alongside while you hand down your traveling case. You come next. Remember, you have to be running forward when you hit the ground. We shouldn't have any trouble."

I perched myself in the open window. Kathy gave me a long, lingering kiss. "Trouble...the two of us?" she said brightly. "Last night we proved that anything we do together ends up just perfect!"

SEVENTEEN

The Hotel Angleterre, despite its exclusive location on the Quai de Mont Blanc, was no longer a first-class hotel. Now more than thirty years old, it showed signs of wear and some neglect. The staff was second-rate as were some of the guests. Kathy and I, somewhat the worse for wear and dressed in slightly rumpled clothes, fit in very well. The Angleterre was endorsed by AXE for personnel wishing to stay in the shadows.

Kathy gave me a mildly disapproving look when I asked for two single rooms with a connecting bath. It was my subtle way of letting her know that we were back on a business-first basis. Her voice was cool when she stuck her head into my room. "Don't you think we'd better let Mr. Hawk know where we are?" she asked. "He'll want to know," she reminded me.

"I'll call him." Kathy might be tempted to give Hawk the complete, uncensored version. Eventually, Hawk was going to learn a lot more than I planned to tell him now. I glanced at my watch. "If there're no delays on an international circuit, I can catch him before he goes to lunch," I thought aloud.

I was lucky. There was only a ten minute delay before my call went through. Hawk made me wait while he got Ginger Bateman on the phone to make notes. "Back in Geneva?" he repeated. "What does that mean?"

"I'm wrapping it up now, chief. The item we want is right here. I should be picking it up today...tomorrow at the latest."

"That's excellent, my boy." Hawk's voice lacked enthusiasm. "Do you expect any interference? Do you need any help?"

"I sidetracked the competition temporarily in Klosters. What I need most is some refinancing to replace lost clothing and equipment and to buy an airline ticket back to Washington. Can you arrange that?"

"Is that all?" Hawk asked with clipped accents.

His voice sounded skeptical. I wondered what Hawk knew and was holding back. "My ETA depends on how soon a flight leaves after I visit a bank and pick up a package left there for Randolph. I'll work up a full briefing on my way back to Washington, sir."

Hawk took his time before speaking again. "I'll want all the facts—all of them. Now, about the money: A bank messenger will deliver two thousand in Swiss francs to your hotel in twenty minutes."

I hung up with the feeling that the exchange was

not one of the warmest conversations I'd had with my boss.

Kathy joined me in the hotel dining room where I was having breakfast and scanning the Berne and Geneva morning papers. Neither mentioned the multiple murders at the chalet near Klosters. They were sensational enough to be newsworthy. The two early editions must have been printed before the police released the story.

Kathy sat looking at me coyly through her long eyeslashes. She was alert and refreshed. Her resilience and stamina were remarkable. "I'd like to explain about—about Leslie and me," she began.

"No explanation necessary," I answered. "I jumped to the wrong conclusion, that's all."

"Well, not exactly, Nick. I moved in with Leslie for a reason. I was through with men. I left my home in Nebraska to take this job in Paris to hide my shame. I was brought up pretty straitlaced and couldn't face my friends after I was dumped by— well, never mind that. I was disillusioned and bitter after a long-running affair—my first. You see, there was just this one guy and it turned sour. It wasn't very good anyway with him—I know that now. But I swore I'd never give myself to another man. So I used Leslie as a bulwark to avoid getting involved with anyone again. Leslie saw that I was lonely and steered clear of men. She took me in, but soon learned I could never be anything but straight. Now we're just friends and roommates. I've lived like a nun for over a year. What I'm trying to say is that last night...until last night...I never...it was never like that for me before."

"You don't have to say anything." I was mildly embarrassed.

"But I do. I want to." Her words spilled out. "I want you to know that you've—well, something I thought was—was buried down inside me has been released and ignited with more intensity than I ever dreamed possible. I didn't know I could respond like—it's hard for me to put it in words, Nick. Please. Just don't leave me. Not yet. Not until I know—until you show me once more—that I'm really capable of—" She stopped, her eyes shining and close to tears.

I was tempted to tell her that there were no frigid women, only inept men. This wasn't the time. "Look, Kathy," I said sincerely, "there's nothing wrong with the way you feel or act. It wasn't a fluke. You're a fantastic woman."

She smiled at that. I watched her dig into a man-size breakfast. I stood up. She put down her fork. "You don't have to hurry off, do you?" she asked. "The banks are going to be open all day. Couldn't we—" She looked toward the elevators suggestively.

I shook my head. "There's a time for everything. Finish your breakfast. Right now I'm going to see the hotel cashier. The bank messenger should have been here by now. I'll pay you back the money I borrowed, then I'm going to get some clothes. While you're waiting, you might call the hospital. Let them know you're coming for a visit. I should be back in an hour."

I bought more than clothes. The new briefcase I carried in my left hand contained an extra shirt, socks and underwear still in cellophane wrappings. Besides the conservative brown suit I wore out of the clothing store, I purchased a knee-length London Fog all-weather coat. Its pockets were large enough to carry the Schmeiser, nine-shot pistol with ease. It was in the right-hand pocket now, its magazine fully loaded. A just-opened box of 9mm. cartridges in the raincoat's left-hand pocket counter-balanced the pistol's weight.

Ste. Moreaux Hospital on Rue de Lausanne was an eight franc cab fare from the hotel. That equated to a rate of four dollars a mile. The white-faced, four-story hospital seemed to be a busy place, efficient and well-staffed. Kathy cut through the red tape runaround. As soon as it was learned that she was responsible for paying the freight on Greta Ulrich's private room, a doctor was summoned. The name tag pinned to his white medical smock read Bocksteger. He was overweight and had a round face masked by a neatly-trimmed full beard and wide-rimmed glasses. His hospital tunic was pulled down on one shoulder from the weight of a stethoscope in its side pocket.

I remained in the background while he had an unsmiling discussion with Kathy. She kept glancing over her shoulder at me. Each time her face appeared more somber. She finally left the doctor and stepped over to me. "I don't know how to explain this. It's not quite the way we thought it would be."

"Greta Ulrich is here, isn't she?"

"Ah, yes. But she's confined to her room."

"Well, that's the way you set it up to make sure she'd be safe," I reminded her.

"Yes, but there's been a complication. The doctor says we should go up to the third floor. Then we'll see."

While we rode in the elevator, Kathy had more

to say. "When I told you we were keeping the Ulrich woman here, all I knew was that she was being held under temporary custody until whatever obstacle to moving her on was eliminated. I figured this was a new kind of safe house concept. The doctor tells me she's here because she actually requires hospitalization."

"Damn!" I sputtered. "That's all we need—having her stuck in a bed recovering from a gall bladder operation or something like that! It could be days before she can walk around and get to the bank."

It was worse than that. Greta Ulrich was in her room sitting in a wheelchair that faced the window. Her back was toward us. The plump nurse—Mme. Dieter according to her name tag—who had escorted us down the corridor spoke gently to her patient. "Greta, you have visitors." Nurse Dieter turned the wheelchair around.

I was shocked. The thin-nosed, pale-faced woman with stringy, grey hair had a slack, twisted mouth and dull, vacant eyes. Her bony hands laying loosely in her lap shook with nervous tremors.

Kathy whispered to me: "I had no idea she was like this."

Nurse Dieter came back and spoke in a low voice. "She was brought in by a very business-like American some days ago." Kathy and I exchanged glances. She nodded silently, confirming that part of the arrangement. "The man left no information other than an address where the bills should be sent," the nurse went on. Kathy nodded again. "Miss Ulrich is Hungarian," Mme. Dieter continued, "and had just arrived in the city to do some banking business. She was able to tell us that much although she complained of headaches and was becoming disoriented. Her main worry was that a letter she had written would not be mailed. I got her an envelope which she addressed and insisted that I mail it before she would get into bed."

"What happened? What's wrong with her?"

"During the night she suffered a mild stroke. The headaches were a warning sign. The cerebral hemorrhage occurred, bringing on aphasia."

"What's aphasia?" Kathy asked.

"Loss of certain mental and motor faculties. She has temporary—possibly permanent—anarthia and agraphia. That's inability to speak and write intelligibly. Other parts of her brain may be affected, but since we can't communicate, we have yet to determine the degree of amnesia normally associated with the disease."

"Will she recover?" was my question.

"She's middle age; that works against her. She's susceptible to another stroke at any time. Barring that, recovery will be slow and rehabilitation an extensive process."

"Does her family know?" Kathy's question was whispered.

"We haven't been able to locate anyone. The letter she wrote to her father was returned as undeliverable. We don't know if there is anyone else."

I was stymied. There was no way this shell of a human being could help me. With those shaky hands, Greta couldn't even feed herself, let alone put a legible signature on a card. Ulrich's formula, for all practical purposes, was going to be locked forever in some bank vault safe deposit box.

Kathy had parallel thoughts, only hers were directed to the pitiful condition of the pathetic wheelchaired figure. "Poor woman," she said softly. "I couldn't stand being like that. Can you imagine having to depend upon others to move you, dress you, comb your hair? Even with partial recovery, she'll have to have someone help prepare her meals, write letters for her, take her places, even use the—"

"That's it!" the thought escaped me, interrupting Kathy. I squeezed her arm gratefully. I spoke louder to Nurse Dieter. "Would it be all right if we stayed a few minutes with Miss Ulrich?"

"Why, of course. It helps her just to know someone is here."

Kathy gave me a questioning frown. When the nurse left, she glanced at the uncomprehending Greta, then confronted me. "She can't communicate. What do you expect her to do?"

"Nothing. She's already done it. We need her identifying signature on a bank card before we can get into the vault and use the key we have."

"I don't understand what you're talking about."

"Greta wrote a letter to her father, remember? Nurse Dieter supplied the envelope and watched Greta address it. The letter wasn't delivered. It came back...back here to the hospital because that was the return address Greta put on it." While I talked, I was going through the drawer of the night stand next to the bed. The envelope with the letter inside was upright between the side of the drawer and an unopened box of facial tissue. In the upper left-hand corner of the envelope was the very legible hospital address topped by Greta Ulrich's name written clearly in bold, firm script.

"What good will that do?" Kathy asked when I showed it to her.

"You said that Greta will need a stand-in to write for her. That's what you're going to do. She won't be able to thank you, but I will—a hundred times over." I tucked the envelope into my jacket pocket and pulled Kathy out of the room after me. In the elevator, I admitted: "Now all I have to do is to find which bank issued the safe deposit box key we have."

During the cab ride back to the hotel, I tore open the envelope. The one-page letter inside was written in Hungarian. It was meaningless to me, although I scanned the words to see if an identifiable bank name had been included. None was. I gave both letter and envelope to Kathy and explained what she must do. As a second priority, she was to man the telephone in case Hawk called. I didn't think he would, although our last conversation had left me uneasy. I sensed that something was bugging him.

Kathy was curious. "You can't just go around the city's financial section asking bank officials if Greta Ulrich has a safe deposit box in their vault."

"No," I answered. "And I'm not going to dangle the key in front of anyone and ask if that's the kind given to box renters, either. I have to be very subtle about it."

It was past three o'clock when I hit pay dirt. Before that I had visited five other banks in the general area Professor Ulrich had indicated as the correct bank's location. I had rented a safe deposit box in each one. Now I was repeating the process in the Geneva branch of the Barclay Bank of England. I listened patiently while the young lady handling my application explained the self-same procedure I had heard five times before. She watched me place my signature on the identity card. "You will sign such a card each time you wish to enter the vault. The signature will be compared to the permanent one kept on file—the one you are signing now. A bank employee with a master key will accompany you to your box in the vault. Each safe deposit box has two locks. Your key will fit one, the bank's master key fits the other. Both keys have to be used simultaneously. Here is your key. Box GM-764."

Finally, after all the keys I'd collected this morning, I found one that looked like the one originally given to Collette.

I recognized both the key shape and the style of the numbers stamped on it. I was elated. My search was at an end. While the accommodating young lady was filing away my signature card, I reached over the counter and palmed three blank cards and stuck them in my pocket. It might make Kathy less nervous to have practiced a couple of times on the real thing.

My high spirits sustained me all the way back to the hotel. If Kathy had done her homework, there was little else left to do. By noon tomorrow I'd be on my way with Ulrich's treasure grasped securely in my weary hands.

I opened the door to Kathy's room, expecting to

find her sitting at the desk, writing. She was gone. I went over to the desk to examine her work. The envelope bearing Greta Ulrich's signature was propped up in plain view. Next to it was a note for me. *Nick: My hand is tired. I need a break. Be back soon. Love, Kathy.*

A dozen sheets of crumpled paper were stuffed into the wastebasket. I picked out the top one. Kathy was making good progress. The last attempts were not perfect, but certainly passable. I deposited the blank signature cards taken from the Barclay Bank on the desk top. The bank's name printed in Old English lettering on the cards reflected the dignified character of the long-established financial institution.

I never knew waiting could be so hard. There have been times when a prolonged absence of a temporary partner would trouble me because of the nature of the assignment. This was different. The danger element was minimal at the moment. Still, I found myself wishing Kathy's note had been more specific.

Unable to bear waiting in the room, I went down to the lobby. I asked the desk clerk if he knew Kathy by sight. All I had to do was describe her eye-catching red hair and her enticing walk. His broad smile told me he hadn't missed the opportunity to ogle her. "Yes, she went out," I was told. "About a half hour ago."

"Alone?"

"Yes, alone."

I returned to my room and paced the floor. I filled the ashtray with stubs of half-smoked cigarettes. I ran through the connecting bath when

I heard Kathy's door open. Her arms were loaded with packages. I was both relieved and miffed. "You should have told me where you were going," I complained.

"I was only shopping," she defended herself. "I was getting writer's cramps. I'm not a professional forger, you know."

"You're doing fine," I relented. "You're almost ready."

"I'm trying," she contended. "I'll practice some more after dinner. I'm having trouble concentrating. I keep remembering—" Her eyes glowed with a devilish sparkle. "It's all your fault, Nick. You've stirred up long-dead desires. I want to be all woman. I even bought new clothes to match my new feelings. All I can think of is how wonderfully close to you I want to be." She started pulling her sweater up over her head.

I backtracked to her bathroom door. "Go ahead and change your clothes," I called out. "When you're ready, come down to the lounge for cocktails. I'm taking you out to dinner. You deserve it. We'll celebrate. I found the bank. Tomorrow we go after the jackpot."

I stopped in the lobby and bought an afternoon newspaper. I carried it to the bar where I perched on a stool and ordered a Jim Beam on the rocks.

The account of the gruesome findings in the Dragner Schloss at Klosters dwelt more on the torture-slaying of a beautiful blonde woman and the condition of her battered, naked body than useful facts. The victims were yet to be identified. Of the two men taken to the local infirmary, the older one had died. The second man, under heavy sedation when examined by a physician, had apparently recovered during the night and left the dispensary without the knowledge of the staff.

I tossed off the Jim Beam in one gulp. Brolaika had slipped away scot-free. It wasn't hard to guess which way he had headed.

I read the rest of the newspaper account. When I saw that the Klosters police refused to comment on the rumor that an American, possibly useful to the investigation, had disappeared leaving his English-made automobile in police custody, I ordered a double from the bartender.

By the time Kathy joined me, I had recovered my composure, but not all of my former confidence. I kept thinking: Brolaika was as inventive as I. He could reach Geneva in no more time than it had taken me. By dawn tomorrow, he could be breathing down my neck. I hoped my sudden gloom would not be detected by Kathy. I shouldn't have worried. She looked so stunning coming toward me that the smile I gave her was genuine and completely spontaneous.

It was near midnight when we returned to the hotel. Kathy was happy. I tried not to spoil her evening by letting my renewed concern show. We had dined by candlelight in the eighteenth-floor restaurant of the International Hotel which provided a superb view of the lake. Afterward, I took Kathy to the lively Ba-Ta-Clan Club with its first-class floor show which included European beauties whose entire costume was a sequined triangle. I was not impressed. None had physical features on a par with Kathy. Her spectacular figure, clothed in a clinging, satiny lime-green dress with a daring decolletage, was far more alluring and provocative than any displayed by the uncovered showgirls. Kathy turned her head and saw that I was admiring her instead of the parading nudes. "I'm ready to leave," she announced. "Let's go back to the hotel. Please?"

In the elevator, I reached for the eighth-floor selector button. Kathy blocked my hand. She stepped in front of me and pushed number twelve. Then she spun around and showed me the room key she had taken from her evening bag. "I stopped at the desk before I came into the bar. We're going to Room 1214. It's got a king-size bed," she beamed. Then she threw her arms around me. The probing kiss she gave me lasted all the way to the twelfth floor.

In the doorway to the room, Kathy plastered herself against me again and smothered me with eager kisses. We never did turn on the lights. Our trail to the huge bed was clearly marked by discarded clothing. When Kathy confessed that her long-curbed passion had been unleashed, she should have posted a warning as well. She should have told me that she intended to catch up on all the sex she had missed in just two unforgettable nights. She demonstrated that a king-size bed permits much more activity and experimentation than a narrow sleeper-train berth.

EIGHTEEN

I rolled out of bed at the break of dawn, as much to avoid an unquenchable Kathy as to prepare for my last day of the job. I left her sleeping and tiptoed out of the room with most of my clothes draped over my arm. At that early hour I had the elevator all to myself.

I knew something was wrong as soon as I opened the door to my original room. Nothing appeared to be out of place, still I tensed, sensing a change. I stood quietly just inside the door trying to detect what had raised my hackles.

Suddenly, I knew what it was. I took a breath, inhaling with short sniffs. I detected the faintest aroma of cigar smoke. Brolaika! His special cigar had left behind traces of his presence. I swallowed hard, thinking how close Kathy and I had come to meeting up with that madman. I blamed myself. I should have killed him when I had the chance.

He had been in Kathy's adjoining room, too. The materials atop the writing desk were undisturbed, but one of the three Barclay Bank customer identity cards I had brought back to the hotel was missing.

Brolaika was as cunning as a rat. The police in Klosters had mistakenly considered Brolaika a victim rather than the prime cause of the Dragner chalet crimes, so obviously no guard had been placed on him. Slipping away and reaching Geneva was no great feat, but his having traced me to the Angleterre Hotel so quickly was wholly unexpected. Brolaika's intrusion into Kathy's room had equipped him with as much knowledge as he needed to forecast my plans. He knew I wouldn't be leaving Geneva before I visited the Barclay Bank.

I used the telephone to awaken Kathy and tell her it was time we got underway. I had shaved and was in the shower when she knocked on the bathroom door. "Do you know what time it is?" she called out accusingly over the sound of spraying water.

"I'll be out in a minute. We've got to get an early start. Pack your things. I want to be at the bank the minute it opens. I've ordered breakfast to be sent to the room."

During breakfast I told Kathy what I had discovered. She agreed that if Brolaika hoped to acquire Ulrich's papers, he couldn't make a move until she had done her impersonation act. Kathy also realized that Brolaika couldn't allow me much running room after she had handed the treasure over to me. The most likely place for the one-man hijacking to occur was in or near the bank.

"Under the circumstances," I said, "I hate to ask

you to go on with what we've planned. Without you, we can't succeed. There's a way to do this that will reduce the risk to you to a minimum. Brolaika has never seen you. As long as we stay apart, he'll never connect you with me. We'll go to the bank separately."

Kathy stopped eating. She gave me a worried look. "Maybe this man knows nothing about me, but if he found Greta's letter to her father and can read Hungarian, he knows everything else."

"Why do you say that?"

"I had lunch downstairs in the dining room yesterday. One of the older waiters is a displaced Hungarian. He read Greta's letter for me. She had written wondering when her father would join her so they could travel to the U.S. She mentioned that some time had passed since he had received the key she obtained after putting an envelope entrusted to her by him into a bank safe deposit box. She reminded him again that the Americans had deposited the promised payment in a Geneva bank, and she was still waiting for the American who is to contact her with the key so the business can be finished. She was disappointed that her father had already been in Switzerland since she was brought to Geneva and had not been permitted to see or call her. She didn't believe there was that much danger or the Americans so restrictive that they couldn't get together for a minute. She closed by saying she was getting anxious and having nervous headaches because of the uncertainties involved."

"It shows how much pressure she was under," I commented. "It clears up a few things for me, too. I never could understand why your planning types back at Langley always make things so damned complicated. Now it's up to you and me to unscramble this barrel of eels." I stared hard at Kathy's lovely face. "There's one small problem. If the bank clerk who processed Greta's initial application for a safe deposit box is checking in vault visitors this morning, you could be in trouble. If you're challenged as an imposter, play dumb. You can talk fast, and I'll be there to confuse the issue."

Breakfast remained a lump in my stomach as I stepped out into the crisp morning air. The hotel doorman hailed two cabs. I took the first one. Kathy, in charge of our luggage, got into the second. Vehicles circling Rond Point de Rive slowed progress, but I was paying off my cab driver within minutes of the bank opening. I delayed crossing the street to allow a sightseeing bus to pass. Its black diesel exhaust fumes welled around me. I took time to pull out a handkerchief and wipe my smarting eyes. It shielded my face while I made a quick survey of my surroundings. I saw nothing out of the ordinary, nor did I expect to. It was up to Kathy behind me to detect the whereabouts of Brolaika.

The bank building was an old granite structure. The sole concession to modernization was the replacement of the original massive wooden portals with a pair of plate glass doors. Each was connected to a pneumatic system that opened them automatically when a customer stepped upon a rubber-mat covered treadle plate. From the curb I could see into the brightly illuminated bank interior the entire length of the spacious lobby. A security guard stood just inside the doors. His middle-aged face was lined, but his eyes were alert.

They lingered on me longer than I liked. He might be recalling having seen me in the pocket-heavy raincoat entering the bank late yesterday afternoon.

I walked the length of the lobby to reach the counter blocking access to the vault situated at the rear of the building. I passed teller's cages on one side and bank officials' desks behind a low balustrade on the other. The terrazzo floor of the lobby glistened from last night's mopping.

The young lady who had waited on me yesterday recognized me. "Good morning, Mr. Carter," she greeted as she placed a bank signature card in front of me. While she searched the file for the master card bearing my original signature, I looked back to see if Kathy had arrived. My eyes ran into those of the bank guard who was watching me. Beyond him and clearly visible through the thick glass doors, Kathy was crossing the sidewalk to enter the bank. The guard turned away from staring at me as the hissing sound of the automatic doors opening for Kathy gained his attention.

"I'll admit you into the vault now, Mr. Carter." The young lady smiled prettily as she accepted the card I had just signed without really looking at it. She pushed a button which unlocked a hip-high gate at the end of the counter nearest the vault door. I stepped through and waited while she unlocked another door of vertical brass bars which was the last barrier to getting into the well-guarded room. She led me to the wall made up of small, burnished steel doors, each containing two keyways. She used my key and hers to open the door to the box I had rented, then withdrew, pointing out the call button next to the entry door to be used when I wished to leave.

I stood where I could see Kathy at the counter. If she was nervous, she hid it well as the vault attendant presented her with a signature card. Kathy's fraudulent autograph was compared to Greta Ulrich's true signature. I relaxed when I saw it passed muster. I turned from the door and carried my empty box to a waist-high work shelf anchored to a side wall.

I kept my back turned while Kathy and the accommodating clerk used their separate keys to gain access to Ulrich's prize. Kathy brought the long, black box over to where I waited. She held her breath as I began to lift its cover. I pushed it back down. "What did you see outside?" I asked in a low voice.

"I think he's out there. A tall man came out of a doorway on the far side of the street and stood behind a parked car just as you went into the bank. He just stood there, watching. It must be Brolaika. I didn't see anyone with him."

"I figured he'd be here," I said flatly. "So let's see what we've got that's so damned priceless." I lifted the box cover. A single, business-size envelope was inside. It was flat and unsealed. Three sheets of thin bond paper were inside. Professor Ulrich had written in a hand that appeared shaky toward the end, but it was all there...a series of seven formulas representing the various steps in the development of his unique substance. In between the formulas was text describing the reactions and technical details as to apparatus and temperatures required.

"Is that all?" Kathy sounded disappointed.

"Big things sometimes come in small packages," I reminded her.

I had one more thing to do before I ran Brolaika's gauntlet. "Stay here and look busy," I told Kathy. "I'll only be a minute."

The bank had a copy machine. The steno pointed out to me left her typewriter long enough to run off single copies of each of the three pages. While I watched her, I felt the bank guard's eyes on me again. His interest in me was annoying. I was re-admitted into the vault without having to go through the rigmarole of signing another identity card. "That's for insurance, in case a duplicate is needed," I explained to Kathy. "You were great. I couldn't have gotten this far without you."

"What you aren't telling me is that I'll be coming back here another time if— Oh, Nick, I don't want to think about it."

"Everything's going to be fine," I assured her without any real personal conviction. In my own mind I didn't know how the unavoidable confrontation with Brolaika could take place without attracting attention. In broad daylight on a busy street, all kinds of witnesses would be present. I didn't think that would make any difference to Brolaika; he was insane and bloodthirsty enough to risk anything in trying to put an end to my existence. Whoever came out of our face off with a whole skin would not escape.

Kathy saw my worried look. "There must be something I can do to help," she begged.

"You can." I stuffed Ulrich's envelope into her shoulder bag. "Take it and walk out of here. Get in the cab you've got waiting and clear out. You know what to do. I'll keep Brolaika occupied. Just don't stop or look back."

"That won't work," she argued sadly. "What I haven't had a chance to tell you is that I saw the man I'm sure is Brolaika walk toward the taxi that brought me. The driver knows that we came out of the hotel together. That we followed you here to the bank. Brolaika must know I'm with you."

Kathy was right. Both of us were in this together. And it was going to take both of us to get one of us out alive.

"I can't stay behind, either," Kathy reasoned. "If something bad happens in front of the bank, the security guard by the door is going to keep everyone inside. I'll be questioned and it will be discovered I'm here under false pretenses. If we have any chance at all of my getting these papers out of the building, I'll have to go first." She had replaced the long black box in the vault wall and shut the small steel door.

I walked over next to her and repeated the performance with the empty box I had. "Wait," I requested. "Give me a moment to think."

I needed longer than that. The germ of an idea blossomed. There was risk, and timing was everything. Kathy kept nodding her head as I described the plan step by step. Then I said: "Ready?" She nodded again. I pushed the wall button to summon the vault attendant. We exited together, but Kathy remained behind making a show of digging around in her purse. I knew she had one eye focused on my back.

I walked through the lobby and stopped just

short of stepping on the rubber mat that activated the automatic door opener. I ran my eyes over the row of automobiles parked parallel to the curb. Brolaika was out there somewhere. He could certainly see me standing in the brightly lit lobby. I had to scan the entire street; he had to watch but one door.

Movement at my left attracted my gaze. Brolaika stepped out from behind a parked car. His act was deliberate. His strange reptilian eyes were cold and unblinking. They glared at me defiantly.

Upon first seeing Brolaika, I had given Kathy a prearranged signal. I knew she was walking across the lobby toward me. I didn't take my eyes off Brolaika. With what was almost a casual motion, he reached into his jacket and drew out a heavy-barreled automatic pistol. From thirty feet away it looked like a miniature cannon. He wasn't going to be subtle about this. From the wild look in his icy eyes, I could tell he was leaving me no choice. Two minutes from now only one of us would be left alive. I jabbed my right hand into the pocket of my trenchcoat and wrapped it around the Schmeiser's pistol grip.

Kathy came abreast of me. I grabbed her around the waist with my left arm. Right on cue, she cried out: "It's a robbery!"

I spun her around so she formed a shield between me and the guard. "Don't anyone move!" I yelled. "Stay right where you are!" The guard reached for his holstered revolver before he saw the shape of a gun in my raincoat pocket. He then moved his hands out to his sides.

I backed onto the door treadle, pulling Kathy with me. My timing was exactly right. The bank alarm sounded at the same instant the pneumatic doors opened. As I had anticipated, an alert employee reacted automatically to the situation. I hoped the bank guard was equally conditioned to respond under stress. If he was, it could be his gun, not mine, that would bring down Brolaika.

The alarm startled Brolaika. It gave me the split-second edge I needed. I shoved Kathy sideways with all my strength. She took three buck-and-wing steps before she tripped over her own feet and fell, sprawling out of the way. I moved in the opposite direction, diving for a niche beyond the hinged side of the door.

The Schmeiser was halfway out of my pocket when Brolaika's first shop zipped past and starred the thick glass door next to me. The second shot came from inside the bank. The guard, seeing Brolaika aiming a gun in his direction, obviously assumed Brolaika was my bank-robbing accomplice staked out to cover my getaway. The guard's shot went wild. Mine didn't. The 9mm. slug plowed into Brolaika's right shoulder. He recoiled from the impact, stepping back between two parked cars. The black pistol dropped from his hand. He backed another step and was stooping to recover his fallen gun when I put a second shot into his left kneecap.

Brolaika slumped to one side and fell backwards out onto the open roadway. I heard the hiss of air brakes and the squeal of skidding rubber. A wide-windowed, glass-canopied tourist bus swerved to miss the prone figure, but Brolaika had tumbled into the street so suddenly that there was no time to stop. I ran forward. In the shelter of a nearby car, I ventured a look back. Kathy was four cars down, walking rapidly across the street to the waiting taxicab. Behind me, the bank guard stood in the open doorway. His mouth was hanging open. Puzzlement shrouded his face.

Brolaika lay ten feet away from me, the centerpiece of a growing pool of blood. One crushed, flattened leg was pinned fast under a wide bus tire. He struggled futilely and weakly, insectlike, to free himself. He was bleeding profusely. Red fluid seeping from his tightlipped mouth indicated extensive internal injuries. He had not yet lost consciousness. He saw me looking at him. Venomous hate flared in his beady eyes until the pain gnawing his life away contorted his features and closed those evil eyes. Somehow I felt nothing—not a single flick of emotion for this soulless creature who deserved every moment of agony to make up for the suffering he had caused others.

Kathy was in the taxicab when I pushed my way through the small crowd of onlookers gathering around the grisly scene. I had to speak to the driver twice to get him to curb his ghoulish curiosity and head for the airport.

Traffic on Rue de la Servette to Cointrin Airport was light. We made good time. I took Kathy to the Air France booking counter and waited with her while the clerk made out the ticket to Paris. "It's over now," she sighed. "Is there any real rush for you to hurry off? I could use a couple of days with you to unwind."

I was saved from answering when my name came

over the paging system. I left Kathy and went to the nearest courtesy phone. A pleasant voice asked me to move to an overseas telephone booth at the east end of the concourse.

It was Hawk, of course. He was in a foul mood. "I've been trying for an hour to get hold of you. You realize don't you, that it's three in the morning here. Well, never mind that. I take it you've finally got what you were sent after?"

"Yes, sir," I replied. "And I have a seat on TWA flight 602 leaving at noon."

"How much did you collect? Is it a big package?"

"Surprisingly little, considering. Three sheets of paper, seven steps, plus some intermediate processing data."

"Can you decipher it?" Hawk snapped.

"I don't have a Ph.D. in chemistry, but I recognize the symbols. The text is handwritten by the professor in English. He apparently was a well-educated man."

"Good!" Hawk's voice brightened. "Very good. And how about Miss Frame?"

I could have made a facetious remark, but Hawk was not making idle conversation. He was leading up to a point. "She was quite helpful," was my censored understatement. "I'm about to ship her back to Paris."

"Don't," Hawk barked. "Listen closely. The papers you have must be destroyed. Got that? Burn them, then flush the ashes down the toilet."

I couldn't believe what he was saying. "You mean—after all I've—after all that's happened, they're fakes—useless?"

"Far from it, Nick. I'm getting ahead of myself. Destruction is step two. Number one is for you and Miss Frame to get off by yourselves somewhere and commit to memory what's on those three sheets of paper. Exactly as written—each word, each symbol. You've got three hours, you say. Knowing you, Nick, and your photographic mind, it should be no chore. You'll have to coach Miss Frame, though. Understand?"

"Yes, sir, I understand. But why involve her? Would it make any difference if you knew our prime competition has been eliminated?"

"That helps, but we still can't risk losing what we've gone through to get. As long as it's in tangible form, it's vulnerable. And it's too vital to be entrusted to one person. So both of you memorize everything and test each other until each of you have it letter perfect. Then get rid of those papers."

I kept quiet about the photostat copy left behind in the safe deposit box. Kathy and I couldn't go back to the bank and be identified with the mess I'd left in the street. I'd have to work that out later. I looked up and saw a sad-faced Kathy standing beside the telephone booth. "Trust me, chief. We've got two hours before the Paris flight leaves. I'll drill it into Kathy before then."

"Hold it!" Hawk's voice rapped. "She's not to go to Paris. She's to come here. Give her your ticket. You'll be taking another flight later. In any event, this situation mandates separate travel to avoid losing both of you should there be an airline disaster with both of you traveling together on the same aircraft."

"Would it be all right if we reversed that order of

departure, sir?" I asked. "For some very good reasons I ought to get out of here as soon as possible."

"If it were up to me, Nick, I'd agree. I've already argued that point and have been overruled. The girl comes first, period. I know what you're up against, which is one reason I'm up at this time of night. Reports are beginning to filter in. The Swiss and the French are now comparing notes, brought about by the mystery of a British Lancia automobile bearing Paris license plates that was abandoned in Klosters. We're doing what we can to slow down Interpol action aimed at finding the person who ran off leaving his car behind. We've gotten our British friends to claim that they picked up a man answering your description at Heathrow Airport and have him in custody. That false scent should give us a few hours grace."

"So what do you want me to do?"

"Something unusual is developing in Pakistan. I need to send someone there to evaluate the situation. A BOAC flight leaves Geneva for Karachi forty minutes after TWA 602 arrives here. If nothing prevents Miss Frame from delivering what's locked in her head, you'll get a call to head east. Get your ticket now and keep a low profile right where you are. You'll be paged by the name of Mr. Knickerbocker."

Kathy and I sat at a table for two in the rear of *Le Petit Café* in the Cointrin Airport terminal for three hours drinking innumerable cups of coffee and memorizing words, sentences and symbols until we knew them better than our own names.

Kathy got to the point where she could recite the complex chemical formulas backwards. The coffee kept my kidneys active.

The fourth time I visited the men's room, I passed up the row of urinals. Instead, I entered a toilet stall. I first lit a cigarette, then kept my lighter going to ignite each one of the three pages containing Ulrich's precious formula.

Kathy and I said goodbye at the TWA boarding gate. Tears brimmed in her eyes.

I don't remember exactly what we said to each other. There were some promises I fully intended to keep. I didn't wait once Kathy got aboard the plane. I turned up my trenchcoat collar and headed for the bar.

**DON'T MISS THE SPECIAL SUPER
VALUE EDITION OF
STRIKE OF THE HAWK
An all-new Nick Carter Thriller
PLUS
DOUBLE IDENTITY
A Second full-length Nick Carter Classic
Adventure!**

There I was, putt-putting in a circle, in a life raft with a leak in it, running out of gas, only two miles off the northern coast of Corsica where everybody, it seemed, wanted me dead, and my only means of escape (or rescue) completely cut off.

To make matters worse, moving lights appeared off to the west, near the corner of the island. I saw two sets. They were the lights of Corsican patrol boats.

The boats were heading toward me.

I knew the consequences. As N3 with AXE, the most secret of all the secret organizations in the world, I knew that I could expect no help from David Hawk, the man who received my reports and gave me my orders, or from the Government I served.

Within minutes after my capture by Corsican Police, especially after what the Corse people must have told them, Paris would be notified and specialists would be sent down. They would find out that I was a Killmaster, the top spy in AXE. They could never torture the information out of me. I have undergone every torture known to man. They would use much more sophisticated means, starting with sodium pentathol, to learn everything that we had spent years keeping secret.

They would try to bargain with Hawk, but Hawk would simply pretend great surprise. I could just see him, pale and tweedy in his Washington office, saying to the French agent sent to make a deal with him:

"Nick Carter? N3? Killmaster? AXE? My dear fellow, I haven't the slightest notion of what you're talking about. Now, if you will pardon me, I must finish this story about the latest Congressional sex scandal and get it on the wire. We are a press service, you know."

AXE, located on Dupont Circle in Washington, uses as a front, the Amalgamated Press and Wire Services. Hawk directs the operations of AXE, actually writes wire stories when he deems it necessary to impress a visitor, and would never admit to any human being in the world that he is anything other than the Washington bureau chief for Amalgamated. Not even under old-style torture.

And the French, finding that I was of no value to

the American organization supposedly known as AXE, would think that somehow I had lied to them in spite of their sophisticated techniques, would figure that I really had gone to Corsica to kill the Governor, and would happily deep-six me in the middle of the Mediterranean.

As the patrol boats came nearer and as my feeling of dejection (and rejection) was hitting bottom, my eyes caught movement in the dark water about thirty feet to my right. A bright yellow ring, a lifebuoy, bounced to the surface.

I turned the liferaft toward it and killed the motor as I came alongside. I pulled my finger from the bullethole in the raft and let the hissing start again. I leaned over and grabbed the yellow circle.

It was attached to a strong, insulated line that disappeared beneath the ocean's surface. As soon as I grabbed it, I almost dropped it, because a tinny voice came from it.

"Take a deep breath and hang on," the voice said from a speaker embedded in the cork circle. Even with the noise of the Corsican patrol boats hauling up on my tail, I recognized the voice as Hawk's.

I slipped the yellow ring over my right shoulder and leaped from the raft. I immediately regretted the action.

The lifebuoy jerked forward so violently that I thought it was going to rip me in two. Water splashed against my face like an unending tidal wave. I turned my head to suck in small gulps of air. Looking back, I saw the big patrol boats circling the liferaft. I didn't see them for long. The yellow ring was streaking along at thirty knots.

In two minutes, which seemed like two years, I was well out of sight of the patrol boats, still being ripped through the water like bait for a whale. My lungs were bursting for a good, deep injection of air, and the bullet hole in my side felt as though it were being torn open by gigantic, fiery hands.

After another five minutes of absolute agony, streaking through the dark, salty Mediterranean, the yellow ring began to slow. It cruised along for another few minutes and then stopped altogether.

Exhausted, I clung tightly to the ring, leaving it snugly anchored over my shoulder. The blasted thing could take off like a jet at any minute. It was vital that I hang on.

Hawk seemed to read my mind. "Glad to see that you're still with us," the tinny voice said. "Hate to go to all this trouble for nothing."

I grinned in spite of the pain and fatigue. I bobbed in the water and waited, grinning. The grin turned into a smile which, in turn, became open laughter. I knew that I was just a bit hysterical, but I was laughing for good reason.

It was the irony of my thoughts at that moment. At a time when I should be grateful for my rescue, grateful for having successfully completed a mission which saved ninety percent of the earth's population—and even remorseful for having had recourse to so much violence—all I could think about was sex.

But the feeling went away when I felt hands reaching for me. Even so, there was still a grin on my face as I walked along the big deck of the Polaris sub, heading for the open hatch, safety and my tweed-jacketed, cigar-smoking, no-nonsense boss.

For this mission, I should get at least a month off. The grin was for all the women I would love during that month.

**from STRIKE OF THE HAWK.
New from Charter in January.**

NICK CARTER

"Nick Carter out-Bonds James Bond."
—<u>Buffalo Evening News</u>

Exciting, international espionage adventure with Nick Carter, Killmaster N3 of AXE, the super-secret agency!

☐ **THE ULTIMATE CODE** 84308-5 $1.50
Nick Carter delivers a decoding machine to Athens—and finds himself in a CIA trap.

☐ **BEIRUT INCIDENT** 05378-5 $1.50
Killmaster infiltrates the Mafia to stop a new breed of underworld killer.

☐ **THE NIGHT OF THE AVENGER** 57496-3 $1.50
From Calcutta, to Peking, to Moscow, to Washington, AXE must prevent total war.

☐ **THE SIGN OF THE COBRA** 76346-4 $1.50
A bizarre religious cult plus a terrifying discovery join forces against N3.

☐ **THE GREEN WOLF CONNECTION** 30328-5 $1.50
Middle-eastern oil is the name of the game, and the sheiks were masters of terror.

Available wherever paperbacks are sold or use this coupon.

CHARTER BOOKS, Book Mailing Service
P.O. Box 690, Rockville Centre, N.Y. 11571

Please send me the titles checked above.

I enclose $_____ . Add 50¢ handling fee per book.

Name_____

Address _____

City_____ State _____ Zip_____

Dc

NICK CARTER
"America's #1 espionage agent."
—Variety

Don't miss a single high-tension novel in the Nick Carter Killmaster series!

☐ **THE JERUSALEM FILE** 38951-5 $1.50
Nick battles Arab terrorists who have kidnapped the world's ten wealthiest men.

☐ **THE FILTHY FIVE** 23765-7 $1.50
Killmaster uncovers a Chinese plot to assassinate the President of the United States.

☐ **SIX BLOODY SUMMER DAYS** 76838-5 $1.50
The search for a stolen nuclear missile sends AXE into a desert death trap.

☐ **THE KATMANDU CONTRACT** 43200-X $1.50
The fate of Asia depended on a billion dollars in diamonds at the roof of the world.

☐ **THE Z DOCUMENT** 95485-5 $1.50
A power-hungry general in the Ethiopian Sahara stops at nothing to dominate the globe.

Available wherever paperbacks are sold or use this coupon.

CHARTER BOOKS, Book Mailing Service
P.O. Box 690, Rockville Centre, N.Y. 11571

Please send me the titles checked above.

I enclose $_____. Add 50¢ handling fee per book.

Name_____

Address_____

City_____ State _____ Zip_____

Ec

"NICK CARTER OUT-BONDS JAMES BOND."
—*Buffalo Evening News*

"Nick Carter is the oldest surviving hero in American fiction. In his latest Killmaster incarnation, he has attracted an army of addicted readers for the Nick Carter series that has been published in a dozen languages, from Dutch to Japanese.... Nick Carter is super-intelligence par excellence ... [his] penchant for sex and violence seems to have universal appeal."
—*The New York Times*

"America's #1 espionage agent."
—*Variety*

"Generation after generation of readers has been drawn to Nick Carter."
—*Christian Science Monitor*

"Nick Carter has emerged as America's most popular, most resilient and most imitated fictional character! . . . Nick Carter is extraordinarily big."

—*Bestsellers*

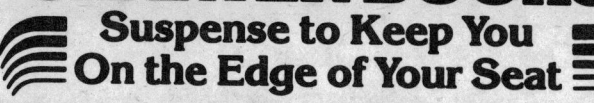

CHARTER BOOKS
Suspense to Keep You On the Edge of Your Seat

DECEIT AND DEADLY LIES
by Franklin Bandy　　　　06517-1　　　　**$2.25**

MacInnes and his Psychological Stress Evaluator could tell when anyone was lying, but could he discover the lies he was telling to himself?

VITAL STATISTICS by Thomas Chastain　86530-5　$1.95

A missing body, several murders and a fortune in diamonds lead J. T. Spanner through a mystery in which New York itself may be one of the suspects. By the author of *Pandora's Box* and *9-1-1*.

POE MUST DIE by Marc Olden　　　67420-8　　　$2.25

Edgar Allen Poe created the modern detective novel; Marc Olden creates Poe as detective in a novel of the occult that the master himself might have written.

THE KREMLIN CONSPIRACY
by Sean Flannery　　　　45500-X　　　　**$2.25**

Detente espionage set in Moscow as two top agents find themselves as pawns in a game being played against the backdrop of a Presidential visit to the Kremlin.

TALON by James Coltrane　　　　79630-3　　　$1.95

The CIA takes care of their own — even if it means killing them. Talon does his job too well and finds himself number one on the hit parade. "One of the year's ten best," TIME MAGAZINE.

Available wherever paperbacks are sold or use this coupon.

C **CHARTER BOOKS** Book Mailing Service
Box 650, Rockville Centre, N.Y. 11571

Please send me titles checked above.

I enclose $ . . . . Add 50¢ handling fee per copy.

Name . . . .

Address. . . . .

City . . . . State . . . . Zip . . . .

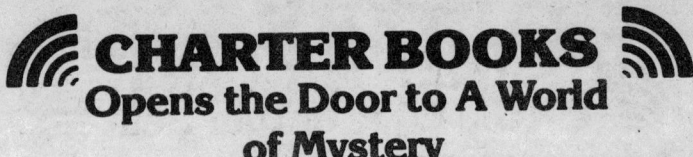

CHARTER BOOKS
Opens the Door to A World of Mystery

Edgar Award Winner Donald E. Westlake
King of the Caper

WHO STOLE SASSI MANOON? 88592-6 **$1.95**
Poor Sassi's been kidnapped at the film festival—and it's the most fun she's had in years.

THE FUGITIVE PIGEON 25800-X **$1.95**
Charlie Poole had it made—until his Uncle's mob associates decided Charlie was a stool pigeon. See Charlie fly!

THE BUSYBODY 68555-5 **$1.95**
First they gave Brody a classic gangland funeral. Then they went to dig him up. The empty coffin didn't do much to make anyone feel secure.

The Mitch Tobin Mysteries
by Tucker Coe

KINDS OF LOVE, KINDS OF DEATH	44467-9	**$1.95**
THE WAX APPLE	87397-9	**$1.95**
A JADE IN ARIES	38075-1	**$1.95**
DON'T LIE TO ME	15835-8	**$1.95**

Available wherever paperbacks are sold or use this coupon.

C CHARTER BOOKS Book Mailing Service
Box 650, Rockville Centre, N.Y. 11571

Please send me titles checked above.

I enclose $...................... Add 50¢ handling fee per copy.

Name ....

Address ....

City.................... State......... Zip ....

Ja